*Harlequin
Presents...*

LILIAN PEAKE

the tender night

Harlequin Books

TORONTO • LONDON • NEW YORK • AMSTERDAM • SYDNEY • WINNIPEG

Harlequin Presents edition published July, 1976
ISBN 0-373-70650-2

Original hardcover edition published in 1975
by Mills & Boon Limited

CHAPTER ONE

AROUND the lily pond, the shrubs, the grasses and rock plants tried vainly in the ruffled waters to find their own reflection. Shelley, elbow on desk, stared out, forgetting for the moment the pile of letters waiting to be answered.

She had not seen the gardens in the summer. It had been October when she had first gone to work at the school. Mrs. Allard, proprietor and headmistress of the small but select educational establishment known as Mapleleaf House School, was a kindly woman. Vague, elusive—she was often away from home—she ran the school, as she put it, without help or hindrance of governors, committees or, she loved to say, any other interfering busybodies.

She was full of sympathy, too, as Shelley, to her immense relief, had discovered on the day of her interview for the job.

Shelley had been running away when she had applied for the post of personal secretary to the headmistress. She had been trying to escape from the ravages of a broken engagement and a shattered heart, a heart so torn in pieces it would have been like trying to fit snowflakes together to form an unbroken sheet of ice. Now she had reached shelter, a haven in which she could hide away and never, ever, be made so unhappy again.

'The man of whom you're thinking,' said a mocking voice from the doorway across the large, high-ceilinged room, 'must surely be out of this world to merit such depth of thought, such a prolonged expenditure of time—and in working hours, too.'

The statement was both a taunt and a reproof and Shelley's head spun round to gaze with unconcealed hostility at the man who had delivered it. The dislike in her eyes seemed to arouse in him a similar response—he, apparently, appreciated being hated on sight no more than any other human being.

He was tall, he was slim and lithe, his hair was black and thick and had a touch of unruliness about it. There were deeply etched lines running from long straight nose to mouth. Expressive eyebrows topped eyes which examined, dissected and anatomsied the girl at the desk who, by now, was feeling like an unfortunate specimen being cut up on a bench in a laboratory.

The path of his thoughts was plain. Shelley could read it in his eyes. This sample of the female of the species, he was thinking, with her tugged-back hair, wearing spectacles totally unsuited to the shape of her face, with a sulkiness about her drawn-in mouth and deep disapproval in those two resentful eyes, was scarcely worth another moment's thought.

As they regarded each other, Shelley could feel the animosity she was offering him being accepted and returned in full measure. There was a war between them, a war which she had instigated and which she was determined to fight to the finish. Who was he, this man who had spoken only a few words to her but who had managed with one sentence to make her hate him on sight?

It did not take her long to make a guess, an accurate guess, as to his identity. If he had not asked a question which gave the secret away, she would have known by the similarity of his features.

'Is my mother around?'

So this was the son of whom Mrs. Allard was so proud. 'I'm sorry, no,' Shelley replied. 'She's gone down to the village.'

'Oh.' He came into the room and stood beside the desk. 'You're her secretary?'

Shelley lifted herself reluctantly from her chair. If this man was the owner's son, she had better show him some deference, even if it irked her so much she felt she would like to pick up the typewriter and throw it at him.

He looked her over swiftly from head to foot and Shelley was conscious of her drab black skirt and white button-up blouse. It was all part of the disguise which she adopted these days to keep any hint of admiration out of men's eyes. She had finished with passion and desire. She had finished

6

with flattering glances and complimentary words. She had finished with men. So she dressed and behaved in such a way as to repel them. No one would believe that under the loose-fitting clothes was a shape which had in the past brought whistles to masculine lips.

'May I know your name?'

'Miss Jenner.'

'Just—"Miss" Jenner?'

Shelley stayed silent.

'Well, *Miss* Jenner, how long will my mother be?'

Shelley looked at her watch. 'I'm afraid I don't know. She was invited out to afternoon tea.'

He frowned. 'In my social circles afternoon tea can be considered to have ended at around four-thirty.' He leaned sideways against the desk and smiled provokingly. 'Tell me what happens in your social circles. It's obvious mine and yours are a world apart.'

'In my social circles,' she returned sourly, 'afternoon tea doesn't exist.'

He folded his arms. 'There seems to be a lot more than afternoon tea missing from your world, Miss Jenner.' His smile merely curved his lips. It did not warm them. 'Pleasantness of manner, politeness in welcoming a stranger——'

'Please forgive me,' she broke in, 'for any lack of courtesy I may have shown, Mr. Allard. I wasn't aware of being discourteous, but if you say I am it must be true.'

There was a fractional narrowing of his eyes and hers shifted uncomfortably from the anger he took no pains to hide. This man, she reasoned silently, was her employer's son. Her newly acquired dislike for men—and oddly, this one in particular—must not be allowed to take possession of her and override her usual good manners. So she apologised again, sincerely this time.

After he had gone, she felt strangely ruffled as if a gale had sprung from nowhere and disturbed her peace of mind —if that was how the state of her mind could be described after Michael had finished with it.

When Michael had walked out on her—they had even bought a house to live in—she had left the firm of engineers for whom she had been working and where he had been employed as a salesman for their products, and had applied for the first job the employment agency had offered. In accepting the post at Mrs. Allard's school, Shelley felt she had taken the most sensible step in her life.

When Muriel Allard had been told by the quiet, rather subdued girl in front of her that she had a younger sister to care for, that they lived in a cramped bed-sitter in one of the less pleasant areas of Newcastle, and that her marriage had been cancelled at the last minute, she had said immediately,

'I can provide you with a house as well as a job. Rent free, my dear. You've enough on your plate without having to pay for a roof over your head. The lodge at the entrance to the grounds has been empty for months. It needs redecorating and a few more bits of furniture, but it's yours and your sister's for as long as you work for me.'

Janine, pretty, appealing, young for her age, which was nineteen, had complained at first. She had objected to the idea of being cut off from the mainstream of life and tucked away on the outskirts of a village in the heart of the North Yorkshire moors. But when Mrs. Allard, having been told by Shelley that her sister was an apprentice hairdresser, wrote and told them that the hairdresser in the village would welcome Janine's assistance with open arms, Janine began to co-operate.

Shelley sighed and walked across the room to look in the mirror behind Mrs. Allard's desk. What had he seen, that arrogant, irritating man who called himself Mrs. Allard's son? Dark hair—as dark as his own—pulled away from a face whose oval shape did not suffer from the consequent exposure, but whose heavy, hopeless expression was revealed all the more clearly to the detriment of the rest of her appearance.

Since Michael had gone out of her life she had forsworn make-up. It only served to attract men, and she wanted no more of that. The clothes she wore had become almost a uniform. She returned to her desk. Why should she care what Mr. Allard—Mr. Craig Allard, wasn't it?—thought of his mother's secretary? He was a man and that made him her enemy from the start.

Mrs. Allard bustled in, a well-proportioned woman with tinted hair and carefully groomed appearance. She was expensively clothed and delicately perfumed and had a busy, breathless manner.

'Your son called in,' Shelley told her at once. 'He was looking for you.' She did not want to be accused by that particular individual of falling down on her job as secretary as well as that of a woman.

'Was he?' Mrs. Allard flipped through the pile of letters on her desk. 'I'm so glad you two have been introduced. I've told him so much about you. He's been abroad for six months. Did I tell you?' Shelley nodded.

'Will he,' Shelley ventured, almost afraid to ask, 'will he be here long?'

'Six months at least,' his mother answered, and Shelley's heart sank without trace. Six months of that man's presence in the house? How could she stand it?

'Did I also tell you,' Mrs. Allard went on, 'he's researching into some aspect or other of education? He's got a year's leave from his senior lectureship at the university and he's writing a book on the result of his researches both at home and abroad. It will keep him quiet. I always think writing a book keeps people quiet—and out of one's way!' She laughed and held out the receiver of the internal telephone. 'Get him for me, dear. Just in case it was important. Extension six.'

I have never, Shelley thought, her fingers busy dialling, hated a number before, but I know I'll grow to hate that one as long as I live! The call was answered.

'Mr. Allard?' she asked crisply. 'Miss Jenner here. Your mother's secretary.'

'Ah, yes,' was the drawled reply, 'Miss Blank Jenner, the lady who wishes to remain half anonymous, whose manners leave a lot to be desired and whose welcome is as warm as an empty grate. But who is, according to my mother, an angel in disguise. Do I trust her judgment or my own?'

'I suggest, Mr. Allard,' Shelley responded icily, 'you reserve your judgment until you know me better.'

'I don't think,' the words came slowly, as if the speaker were considering them carefully, 'I want to get to know you better, Miss Jenner. I can see nothing advantageous in it for either of us, can you? Put me on to my mother, please.'

Shelley thrust the receiver towards Mrs. Allard as if it had grown red hot in her hand. Mrs. Allard took it absently, her mind on other things.

'Yes, dear? Shelley—a *she-dragon*? My dear boy, she's the sweetest, most charming...' The laughter from the other end was so loud Mrs. Allard was forced to hold the receiver some distance from her ear. Then, 'But, Craig, you've got her all wrong. Yes,' with a frown, 'that's her name. Shelley, Shelley Jenner. She wouldn't tell you? Oh, I expect she was too shy.' More laughter from the vibrating piece of equipment in Mrs. Allard's hand.

'Why did you want me?' Muriel Allard asked her son. 'You've got a spare ticket for a dance in the village? Where, at the Wallasey-Brownes'? I suppose it's a charity affair arranged, no doubt, by Sylva. You're offering the ticket to my she-dragon? Well, she's not usually a party kind of girl. Her social life is non-existent. What did you say? With a personality like hers you're not surprised? Oh, you're wrong, Craig! You think I'm prejudiced, you'd rather believe the evidence of your own eyes? Now you've annoyed her, dear, I can see how angry she is with you.' Another burst of laughter, full of mockery, came from the headmistress's son. 'After that,' his mother said, 'I doubt if she'll accept that ticket. Wait a minute, I'll ask her.'

Shelley had been awaiting with anticipation for the moment when she would have the pleasure of flinging Mr. Craig Allard's gracious offer back in his face. But she remembered Janine. The poor girl, she reflected, had virtually no social life, either. Why condemn her to the withdrawal from society which she had imposed upon herself? Yes, she would accept the ticket for Janine's sake. Shelley nodded, but a few moments later regretted the action wholeheartedly.

Mrs. Allard said, 'She'll take it, Craig. My word, you don't know how honoured you are to lure Shelley from her hermit-like existence. She seems to have built her own impregnable castle around her and no man, no man whatsoever, she says, is going to be allowed to storm it! Will

10

you bring it down, dear? Oh, you want Shelley to come for it? But, Craig, it's a long way up those stairs.' She listened. 'If not, she doesn't get it?' Mrs. Allard frowned. 'That's a little unkind of you, isn't it?'

Shelley turned away, hiding her crimson cheeks. She wished she had said 'No, thank you' a thousand times over.

'He has three rooms on the top floor, dear,' Mrs. Allard said, replacing the receiver. 'I'm so sorry I couldn't persuade him to bring it down. He has his awkward side, just as his father had, dear man, when he was alive. I kept telling William, my late husband, "Don't leave me Mapleleaf House in your will, darling, because the upkeep of it will be so great, and anyway you know I never like being tied down to one place." But he did leave it to me, the darling, so I gave it to Craig on the spot, provided he didn't object if I opened a school—a lifetime's ambition of mine —and paid for the upkeep that way. He said if that would make me happy, go ahead. So I went ahead. He's a good son, even if he does have as many prickles on him as a hedgehog. And this is an example of his prickles, his insistence that you go all the way up four flights of stairs to collect a ticket for a dance. Do you mind going, dear? I'd send one of the children, but Craig objects to them wandering about in the private section of the house.'

Shelley lied, clenching her fists, 'No, I don't mind at all, Mrs. Allard.'

Four flights, each flight with two sections to it ... if it weren't for Janine, she told herself, she would tell Mr. Craig Allard what he could do with his ticket for the dance.

Three doors, each of them panelled and varnished, each of them as daunting as the other. There came the sound of tapping from the room at the end of the corridor, the sluggish, painstaking tapping of keys pressed by someone unfamiliar with the art of typing.

The answer to her knock came loudly if tersely and Shelley entered. The room was spacious and airy, more like an artist's studio than a bedroom which, two centuries before, must have been its function.

Now it was a living-room with an expensive-looking leather-upholstered suite arranged around the fireplace, and

11

a circular table near a small window. The other end of the room had been furnished with office equipment. A filing cabinet stood in a corner with its drawers half opened, in-trays and out-trays rested side by side on a desk. Reference books were piled high to one side of it and papers were scattered untidily about the desk top.

The lack of order offended Shelley's trained secretarial mind and if she had not disliked so intensely the man to whom the desk belonged, she wouldn't have been able to stop herself from getting down to the job of tidying it there and then.

He saw her hurt expression—it produced something very like a physical ache in her hands and fingers having to re-strain them from reaching out to restore order—and he laughed.

'So the bespectacled she-dragon is upset by the chaos? Let me tell Miss *Shelley* Jenner at the very beginning of our acquaintance that I'm not going to allow her within breathing distance of it. If there's one thing I cannot stand it's efficient secretaries. They stifle a man, hedge him in, pester him to death like an overdeveloped conscience. This chaos,' his hand moved, 'is the garden from which my choicest thoughts grow. Originality can't thrive in a strictly controlled, over-disciplined atmosphere.'

'I assure you, Mr. Allard,' Shelley muttered, 'that all I want to do is to get out of this room as fast as my feet will take me.'

His eyes flickered. 'I'm making you a gift, Miss Jenner,' he said, his voice abrasive. 'The ticket has been paid for, by me. I'm not asking you for the money.'

She coloured uncomfortably. 'If I had my purse here I'd——'

'And I would say no, thank you.' Slowly, as if delib-erately keeping her waiting, he took out his wallet, went through its contents and extracted the ticket. This he threw across the desk. It landed in the out-tray. Shelley moved to pick it up, but checked herself and looked at him. He looked back at her questioningly. The careless way he had given it to her called for retaliation in kind.

'The ticket, Miss Jenner.'

Her hands went behind her back. 'I'm not going to be allowed within breathing distance of your chaos, Mr. Allard. You said so yourself, so you surely wouldn't expect me——'

His chair made ridges in the pile of the carpet as he pushed it back and got to his feet. He picked up the ticket, eyed the neck of her blouse and said, 'I've a damned good mind——'

Her hand came out quickly and he smiled. His threat, which he looked quite capable of carrying out if provoked far enough, had nullified her revenge as if it had never existed. For a few moments he kept her in suspense, as if enjoying the humiliation she was feeling in standing before him with her hand outstretched in mute pleading, then he seemed to relent and the ticket was passed over the desk.

'You would do well, Miss Jenner,' he advised, 'to keep your fangs well hidden when I'm around. You may wind my mother round your little finger, but no woman, not even a frustrated, acrimonious she-dragon, has ever been allowed to push me in whatever direction she fancies.'

Their eyes met and there was anger—even hatred—in the look that passed between them. If she had dared, Shelley would have torn the ticket into pieces and thrown them at him.

When the door closed behind her, Shelley rested against the banister, breathing as deeply as if she had been running for her life.

Mapleleaf Lodge, in which Shelley and her sister Janine lived, was at the end of the long, winding drive, and overlooking the entrance gates. It took Shelley the length of that drive to calm down. It was not only the cold wind sweeping across the lawns and gardens which had her gripping the collar of her coat. She was still smarting from her encounter with the owner of the house.

The lodge was constructed of stone with slated roof and a shaded porch. In summer the walls were laden with climbing flowers and the roof of the porch spilled over with them. Although the calendar indicated that spring was near, there was not even the sign of a bud, and the barrenness

13

found an answer in Shelley's empty heart.

The gate creaked on its hinges, telling of the need for a touch of oil. The thick wooden door opened on to a miniature hall and the living-room was an almost perfect square, with the faintest echoes of the grandeur of the great house over which it stood guard.

Before leaving for work that morning, Shelley had cleared the grate and built up the logs for the evening's fire. The match caught the newspaper and flames rose and curled round the wood, creating a sweet, pungent smell.

The evening bus from the town trundled away down the road and a few minutes later Janine came in. Her bright smile, her round, pretty face, the curls which clustered over her head, left an onlooker in no doubt as to the cheerfulness of her disposition. Shelley thought with affectionate amusement, Jan looks like everyone else's sister but mine.

Comparing the two girls, people had often remarked that they might have come from different moulds, both in looks and personality. Shelley was serious and knowledgeable; Janine the lively, attractive one with nothing to boast about where the contents of her brain were concerned. But give her a head of hair and her magic fingers could work wonders.

Janine had often eyed her elder sister's hair with longing, but Shelley consistently refused to let her so much as comb it. Once she had looked attractive—beautiful even, some said—for Michael. After what he had done to her, she had vowed never to look attractive for any man again.

Janine took the ticket for the buffet dance with a whoop of joy. 'Tonight? At Shurwood Hall? I know it. Sylva Wallasey-Browne lives there. She comes to the shop sometimes to get her hair done when her own hairdresser in town is indisposed, as she puts it. So it's at the beautiful Sylva's house.' Janine waved the ticket. 'This is the only way someone like me can get into the residences of those rich "county" types. Who's paying?'

When Shelley told her the cost of her outing was being borne by none other than the owner of Mapleleaf House himself, she whistled then frowned. 'But if he gave it to you——'

14

Shelley said she had better tell her little sister the facts of life regarding her own relationship with that horror of a man called Craig Allard. 'But,' Janine protested, 'you only met him today. How can you hate each other already?'

'I don't know, Jan. We just do. Put us within the same four walls and the air crackles, like the radio when there's a thunderstorm about!'

Shelley spent a quiet evening repairing her own and Janine's clothes. Although they lived rent-free, their style of living was simple. It had to be. Shelley's salary was not high, and Janine, as a trainee hairdresser, did not bring home a great deal of money.

It was impossible for Shelley to concentrate for long periods on the television. Her imagination kept detaching itself and floating away to hover, like a spy satellite, over the great country mansion known as Shurwood Hall.

Into her mind came pictures of dancing—no doubt there was a large drawing-room in the house. All the great residences of the past had them, hadn't they? That was probably where the dance was being held. And Janine was enjoying herself, of that Shelley could be sure. Her sister's nature was such that no matter what the circumstances, her spontaneity and joy of living would touch and enliven whoever was with her.

And who was Janine's partner? Craig Allard? After all, he had provided the ticket. Or perhaps it was his own ticket he had given away? Was he perhaps not the social creature he appeared to be? Did he, like Shelley, prefer the quiet life, leaving the socialising to others more inclined for it?

From her short if stormy acquaintance with the man, Shelley was convinced that this was not the case. There was an air about him of self-reliance, of someone accustomed to mixing easily with his fellow men. Not, Shelley thought wryly, to mention women. If any man had the measure of womankind, it was Craig Allard.

She looked at her watch and her imagination shifted and hovered again. There would be food, on long trestle tables, no doubt; savouries, rolls, tantalising the eyes and exciting the appetite. She could almost smell the coffee, almost hear the talking and the laughing. So strong was the impression

15

that she closed her eyes and felt she was there amongst the crowds, invisible, unheard, laughing, talking, glowing with conviviality and happiness.

Shocked by the treachery of her subconscious mind, Shelley put aside her sewing and with an irritable twist of the fingers, turned off the television. That, too, had been offering her a means of escape, but it was the wrong route into dreamland. That route was a dead end. The path on which her mind had been leading her had, to her dismay, proved far more inviting.

What was the matter with her? Was she longing again for the bright lights, for involvement, for the pleasures she thought she had so successfully put behind her after the trauma of losing Michael had worn off, leaving her self-respect a ruin and allowing the dust of disillusionment to settle, like a permanent shroud, over her personality?

She would have a bath and as soon as Janine came home she would make her a milk drink and go to bed. Someone, she was sure, would walk Janine home—Janine would see to that. She belonged to the village tennis club and some of its members must have been at the dance.

Shelley decided to wash her hair. Afterwards it spread in a dark cloud over her shoulders, softening her features and touching her expression with a winsome, elusive sadness. The lingerie she had bought for her wedding and her honeymoon was six months old. Now she wore the garments every day, putting ruthlessly out of her mind all the meaning and the promise they had once held.

As the soft transparency of her nightgown drifted past her shoulders to reach just below her knees, and the negligée, pale blue, covered her body and fell in a deep frill to sweep the floor, she caught sight of herself in the mirror. For the first time in six months she looked at herself frankly, and equally frank were her thoughts—about her broken relationship with her fiancé and about herself.

She thought, Michael never saw me like this. I never let him get beneath my surface. The connotations of the words 'her surface' caught at her mind and she made a wry face, remembering how she used to repel Michael's approaches. Wait, she had said, wait until—until what? she asked her-

16

self harshly. Until the ring was on her finger and the marriage certificate in her hand?

Relief swept over her as the key turned in the front door. Janine was home. Her self-examination was at an end. The sense of reprieve which flowed over her turned on a light in her face and she hurried down the stairs to greet her sister. But her sister was not alone.

Craig Allard was beside her, gazing up the stairs at the girl who, her face drained of colour, her hand over her mouth, stood halfway down the staircase watching them come in.

CHAPTER TWO

JANINE said 'Hi!' and broke the silence. Then she said, pointing at Craig as if she had won him at a fair, 'Look who I've brought home. He was my partner.'

Slowly, the negligée trailing behind her like the train of a wedding dress, Shelley descended the stairs. Her cheeks, which a few moments before had been white, were now scarlet—with embarrassment, confusion and, strangely, with anger. How dared Craig Allard invite himself into their home? She quite overlooked the fact that it was her sister who had invited him. He was her sworn enemy and could therefore do no right.

'He's come for coffee,' Janine raced on, blind to the undercurrents. 'He danced with me all the evening, Shelley.' She gazed with rapture into Craig Allard's face. 'He said if you had gone, he would have danced with you.'

'How very kind,' Shelley murmured. Judging by the flick of his eyebrow, Craig had detected the sarcasm.

'Take Mr. Allard into the sitting-room, Jan,' Shelley directed. 'I'll make some coffee.'

'No, no,' Janine pushed Craig and her sister along the hall. 'I'll make it. I promised, didn't I, Craig?'

They were alone in the centre of the living-room. 'I'm sorry, Mr. Allard,' Shelley said.

Craig frowned, rubbed the back of his neck and shook his head. 'You have me there, Miss Jenner. For what are you apologising?'

'For—for——' She looked down at herself.

'For your appearance? My dear Miss Jenner,' now there was sarcasm in his voice, 'I can't fault it. I came prepared to brave the she-dragon in her lair, and what do I find? That she's wriggled out of her reptilian skin and has turned into a human being after all! She's transformed into a woman. Come to work dressed like that, spend all your days dressed like that. I should be the last to complain!'

The lodge was small and voices carried. Janine, in the kitchen, overheard. 'They're her wedding clothes,' she called. She appeared at the door, coffee pot in her hand. 'Shelley was going to be married, didn't you know? Michael phoned the day before the wedding and said he couldn't go through with it.'

Having delivered her time-bomb on the doorstep, she went away.

'Now,' Craig breathed, 'I get the picture. Jilted bride swears vengeance on all men because the man she loved deserted her.'

Shelley sank into an armchair, while Craig dropped into the chair on the other side of the hearth. 'My opinion of men, Mr. Allard,' Shelley said, 'of their integrity and faithfulness, is my concern and no one else's.'

Craig inclined his head mockingly. 'Too true, Miss Jenner. It certainly won't keep me awake at nights wondering what you think of me.'

Shelley tightened her lips, noticed the fire was in need of more coal and knelt on the hearthrug. But Craig was out of his chair and, with his hands on her shoulders, eased her away. 'Allow me, Miss Jenner,' he said, with mock courtesy.

With an irritable movement she freed herself from all contact with him. That he did not like the way she shrank from him was plain from the narrowing of his eyes, but he made no comment, bending down to lift a log on to the dying embers and sending sparks spurting up the chimney.

Coffee cups rattled their way along the hall and Janine, eyes bright, mouth stretched in a carefree smile, stood in the doorway and took a deep breath. 'Mm, coffee! After an evening of breathing in expensive perfumes and cigarette smoke, this smell beats the lot. I'll pour, Shelley.'

As she handed Craig his cup, Janine said, 'Now you know what my sister would have looked like on her wedding night.'

'Janine!' Shelley reproved sharply.

Half-closed eyes contemplated the filmy blue. 'Yes, Janine, in the outfit she's wearing, it's not at all difficult to visualise your sister on her wedding night.'

19

Shelley flushed, the scarlet flames turning her cheeks to an even deeper shade of red. She pulled the frills around her neck a little closer and challenged angrily, 'Do you think I dressed like this for your benefit, Mr. Allard? If so, I must correct that impression. I didn't invite you in. In fact, if I'd known you were coming, I would have locked myself in my bedroom and not come out until the front door had been bolted against you.'

The anger in his eyes was veiled but unmistakable. His fingers drummed lightly on the arm of the chair. Janine laughed, feeling the tension.

'Shelley hates men, Craig,' she said, 'and all because of Michael Townley. She was crazy about him. When he ran away from marrying her, she broke her heart. She didn't stop crying for days. She says she's never going to fall in love again.'

Faintly Shelley said, 'Jan, please stop.'

But Janine went on unperturbed. 'She swears she's never going to get married, but even if she doesn't she needn't worry. She's bright, not like me. I'm so dim all I can do is wash women's hair.'

'It's not true, Jan,' Shelley corrected, putting down her empty cup. 'One day you'll make a wonderful hairdresser. If we can find the capital—save up our earnings—in a few years you'll be able to open a shop of your own.'

'You're a hairdresser, Janine?' Craig asked, tipping the remainder of his coffee down his throat.

'I'm training to be one. I've three months to go before I take my final exam.' She turned excitedly to Shelley. 'Mrs. Caversham said today that when I'm qualified she'll offer me a partnership, provided I can put enough cash into the business.' Janine curled up on the rug in front of the fire. 'Do you think we'll be able to, Shelley?'

Shelley looked doubtful. 'Money's a bit tight, Jan. My salary isn't——' She glanced uncomfortably at Craig.

'Isn't what, Miss Jenner?' he asked tersely.

Confused, Shelley tried to cover her mistake. 'I'm—I'm happy in my job, Mr. Allard. I came to work for your mother with my eyes open. I knew how much she would be paying me.'

'Don't you mean "how little"?' He looked around. 'I believe you get this place rent-free?'

'I'm not complaining, Mr. Allard,' she said desperately, 'please believe me.' Now what had she done—jeopardised her job by a mere slip of the tongue? 'Please promise you won't say anything to your mother...' His face was impassive. 'I love my work, Mr. Allard——'

He moved impatiently. 'What do you think I'm scheming to do? Have you dismissed because you dared to mention— no, you dared to *think*—that your salary is low? What sort of a brute do you think I am?'

Janine said joyfully, 'It's because she hates men so much, Craig. She can't help being nasty to them.' She turned quickly to Shelley. 'If we can't find the money perhaps Emery could help us out. We could promise to pay it back. She told Craig, 'Emery's Shelley's boy-friend.'

Craig rose lazily and stood with his back to the fire, looking down on the two sisters. 'I think,' he said, with an irritating smile, 'it's time we had a recap. You've got me confused, Janine. First you tell me your sister's heart has been broken and that she consequently hates men. Second, she's never going to get married, and yet,' he gazed at Shelley with mocking astonishment, 'third, she has a boy-friend. One of us is surely crazy?'

Shelley broke in defensively, 'She's wrong, Mr. Allard. Emery Slade is a *friend*, no more, no less. There's nothing between us, not in the sense Janine's implying. As far as I'm concerned, there couldn't possibly be.' She pressed a hand to her ribs. 'Inside I'm—I'm dead.'

'Then isn't it time,' he murmured derisively, 'you buried yourself—away from all *man*kind?'

He held out a hand to Janine, hauling her up. 'Thanks for your company this evening,' he said. 'Don't ever let yourself grow bitter and unlovable like your sister. I should hate to see those two bright eyes turned into muddy, chilling pools.' He held Janine's shoulders, brushed his lips over hers and said, 'See me out?'

With a low, mocking bow he said, 'Goodnight, Miss Jenner. Thank you for giving your sister the ticket I gave you. By being so self-sacrificing you've saved me from passing a

21

dull evening in dull company.'

As he went out, pulling Janine behind him, Shelley found to her horror that her lip was trembling. She wanted to run after him, pound him on the back and say, 'A man loved me once, enough to want to marry me, so I can't be as bad as you seem to think I am.'

Janine returned, her face radiant. 'He's asked me out again tomorrow evening. You don't mind, do you, Shelley? I know you don't like him, but——'

'Of course I don't mind, Jan,' Shelley assured her with a strained smile. 'Anyway, even if I did you're old enough now to go your own way.'

'He's nice,' Janine sighed. 'He was a fabulous partner. He's a dream. He's so much more—more mature than the boys at the tennis club.' She sat in the armchair Craig had vacated. 'Sylva Wallasey-Browne was there, of course. She kept hanging round him trying to make him ask her to dance. He did, a couple of times.' Janine closed her eyes. 'I did hear someone say he used to be friendly—more than friendly—with her, but a year or so ago everything between them seemed to come to a stop.'

Shelley said irritably, 'Take my advice, Jan. Don't fall for that man.'

But Janine smiled seraphically. 'He's a dream,' she repeated. 'I could fall for him *hard*. In fact,' she sighed and stretched, 'I think I'm already halfway there.'

Mapleleaf House School catered for boys from five to thirteen years of age. There were about two hundred pupils at the school, half of them boarders, the rest coming daily from nearby towns and villages, sons of farmers, industrialists and wealthy townsfolk.

The house itself stood, surrounded by its own estate, on the edge of the Cleveland Hills, with heather-covered moorland reaching almost to its doorstep. In front of it was a curving drive linking with the main road, and connecting the house and its inhabitants with the industrial towns of north-eastern England. To the east were the rocky bays and inlets of the coast.

Mapleleaf House was unusually tall for a country mansion. In appearance it was satisfyingly symmetrical. The entrance door was exactly central, two tall chimneys rose like elongated rabbits' ears from the roof and between them, on the fourth floor, were three gabled attic windows which marked the suite of rooms occupied by Craig Allard.

The building had the appearance of a dolls' house. It was high and narrow. In the early nineteenth century it had been owned by a man grown rich with the wealth he had acquired from the beginnings of the industrial revolution. He, too, had apparently thought, with its symmetry and height, it had resembled a child's plaything. History had it that he objected to living in a 'house made for dolls' and, using some of his accumulated wealth, had set about providing himself with more living space.

So two more buildings were erected, three storeys high and again exactly symmetrical. It was these two buildings which now provided living and sleeping accommodation for the young boarders and also for those members of staff who were in residence. It was in the main building that classes were held. It was also where the headmistress, Mrs. Allard, lived in grace and comfort and administered the running of the school.

As Shelley arrived for work the morning after Craig's visit to the lodge, he came down the stairs into the wood-panelled entrance hall.

He frowned at his watch and Shelley said defensively, 'I'm not late. If anything, I'm early.'

'Are you?' he asked disinterestedly. 'Where's my mother?' He followed Shelley into the headmistress's office.

Shelley removed her coat and scarf and hung them in a cupboard. 'Probably with Matron. She has a talk with her every morning to discuss the health and welfare of the boys.' Shelley took her spectacles from her case and put them on. It was easier to withstand the impact of the owner of Mapleleaf House with two pieces of glass in front of her eyes.

'Where's the deputy headmistress, Miss—I've forgotten her name?'

'Miss Feather. She left us three months ago. Your mother hasn't replaced her yet.'

'So who does her work?'

Shelley uncovered the typewriter, opened various drawers and took out pens, pencils and sheets of paper. It was a good way, she felt, of dodging the question.

Craig was not fooled. He asked suspiciously, 'Not you?'

She refused to give a direct answer. 'I help your mother in every way I can.'

He came towards her. 'You're not telling me that in my mother's absence you even deputise for her?'

She said primly, busying herself with opening letters, 'To the best of my ability.'

'But with due respect, you're hardly the right person. Neither are you paid the right salary. If my mother permits this, not only is she exploiting you, she's breaking the rules. And, what's more, failing to give the fee-paying parents value for money.'

Shelley looked at him with defiance. 'And you know all about education.'

'Yes, Miss Jenner,' crushingly, 'I know a great deal about education. I should do, since I not only hold a master's degree on the subject, but I lecture on it, too.'

These items of information shook her to the extent of making her sink into her chair. 'You're a——' she looked up at him uncertainly, 'you're a specialist in the subject? You're an M.Ed., a Master of Education?'

He inclined his head. 'But,' sardonically, 'don't let it keep you awake at nights.'

She coloured under the sting of his sarcasm and gathered up her belongings. He watched her make for the door. 'Where are you going?'

'To——' Should she tell him? 'To—take a class.'

Slowly, unbelievingly, he crossed the room. 'To *what*?'

His anger unsteadied her legs as well as her tongue. 'To —to teach.'

'But you can't. You're not qualified. Are you?'

She shook her head.

'So what goes on in this school? What does my mother think she's up to? Am I permitted to ask which subject you're going to "teach"?' He smeared the word with mockery.

She opened and closed her handbag uncomfortably. 'The woman who teaches the youngest children to read is away ill. Whenever that happens I take over.'

'Does it happen often?'

She flashed at him, 'Are you a member of the teaching inspectorate in disguise? Or a spy for them, perhaps?' But she regretted her words immediately.

His expression, full of anger, forced an apology from her.

He asked sharply, 'Does this—this charade happen often?'

'Mrs. Gordon is away fairly often, yes. She has an ailing mother.'

'So Miss Shelley "office girl" Jenner changes hats and becomes Miss Shelley "schoolmarm" Jenner, inexperienced, untrained, her only asset being her willingness to get her employer out of an awkward situation.'

'Thanks for the compliments,' she responded sourly, 'but you've overlooked another of my assets. I happen to love children.'

'Love of children is an emotion. It's hardly a qualification which the teaching fraternity looks upon as a hallmark of teaching skill.'

It was time, she thought, to defend herself from this man. 'I get results. If you don't believe me, come and listen.'

He looked her over and there were no compliments in his eyes. Shelley became conscious of her drawn-back hair and colourless cheeks. She recalled his words to her sister the night before which told her, Shelley, exactly what he thought of her appearance and personality.

'So now,' he said unpleasantly, 'having in a roundabout way accused me of professional spying, you invite me to sit in on your class? That, Miss Jenner, is an invitation I intend to accept.' His hand indicated the door. 'Lead the way.'

There were eight five-year-olds in the class, eight small boys, well fed and cared for, nurtured on near-luxury at home and with every physical comfort at school. At the moment they were running about the schoolroom, and it echoed with their shouts.

When Shelley appeared in the doorway, they surrounded her and fought to be the favoured ones to sit beside her. It was difficult to shut her mind to the presence of the man she had unwillingly invited to supervise her lesson, but with a supreme effort she managed it. While she sat amongst the semi-circle of lively, bright-minded children, Craig pressed his back against a windowsill and stood with folded arms and a sardonic expression, blocking out a large portion of daylight.

As Shelley listened to the children's efforts to read, some of them halting, some remarkably fluent, a thrill of triumph ran through her and she stole a defiant look at the spectator. But he was contemplating his shoes at the end of his crossed legs with a detached, unreadable expression. Certainly there was no praise in it for her achievement.

During the lesson, which lasted half an hour, he wandered about, studied the words on the blackboard, gazed out of the window and at last sat cornerwise on the teacher's desk, swinging his leg. All the time Shelley felt he was listening, that he had not once allowed his attention to wander from the teacher and her eager young pupils. But what annoyed her most was that, no matter how many times she glanced at him, she could not tell what he was thinking.

The children scampered away along the corridor to their next class and Shelley prepared to leave the schoolroom.

'Perhaps,' she murmured, smiling and deliberately provoking, 'you found it hard to descend to the abysmally low level of children learning to read? Maybe you've become so accustomed to the pinnacle of learning you occupy in the academic world, you can't stoop low enough any more to appreciate the difficulties of those at the bottom of the educational ladder?'

'If I were you, Miss Jenner,' he spoke quietly, 'I should not set out to annoy, I should subside unobtrusively into a corner and put on a fur coat to counteract the effects of the cold, cold criticism which might come your way.'

'But,' she said, bewildered, 'what did I do wrong? You heard how fluently those children read, although the oldest was only five and a half.'

'All right, so they could read. Who taught them last week?'

'Mrs. Gordon.'

'And the week before that?'

'Mrs. Gordon. But she was away the two weeks prior to that.'

'And Mrs. Gordon is a qualified teacher?' Shelley nodded. 'Then it's Mrs. Gordon who should take the credit, not you. All you did was, educationally speaking, baby-sit. You merely heard the results of Mrs. Gordon's work.'

So he was not even prepared to give her the credit of teaching one single new word to those children! She said, defiantly, 'But as you said, Mr. Allard, I'm not a real teacher, so what did you expect? And as you said, I'm not paid a teacher's salary, so did you really expect me to put myself out?'

She flounced out of the room, ran down the stairs and burst into Mrs. Allard's office. To Shelley's disappointment, the headmistress's chair was still empty. Craig Allard followed her all the way. He had not finished with her.

'I'm sorry,' he said, 'but you had no right to take that class. It was against all the rules. I shall speak to my mother about it. A secretary teaching children to read! No local authority would tolerate such an arrangement, let alone the teacher's trade unions. In some schools there would be a strike on the headmistress's hands.'

Shelley felt like crying. 'Thank you,' she said bitterly, 'for your gratitude to me in helping your mother out, for taking time off from my secretarial duties and for—for letting my work pile up and getting behind for the rest of the day . . .'

'All right, you've made your point. I'll write you a formal letter of thanks.'

'There's no need for that,' she snapped, goaded by his sarcasm. 'Just keep out of my way, that's all, Mr. Allard.'

She knew she had broken not only the rules of politeness, but was even endangering her job by speaking in such an insubordinate way to her employer's son—the man, in fact, to whom the great residence belonged—but she did not care. She would get this man off her back even if as a result she found herself applying to the town's employment bureau for another job, even if he threw her and her sister out of their home. This, as she was aware, he was quite entitled to do.

He said frigidly, 'I appreciate the sentiments behind the order you've just given me, Miss Jenner, but unfortunately I can't promise to act upon it. If I wanted to sit there,' indicating his mother's chair, 'with my feet up on that desk, watching you all day and tearing your work to pieces, I could do just that. Remember that, the next time you feel like flinging your spite and bad temper in my face.'

Shelley sat at her desk and inserted some paper into the typewriter. The door opened and a head came round it. A tall, thin young man stood in the doorway and seemed to be wondering whether to advance or retreat. Shelley, delighted at his timely appearance, stretched out her hand.

'Emery,' she said, 'come in.'

As he walked past Craig Allard, he eyed him like a student demonstrator eyeing a policeman, and sat himself awkwardly on the edge of Shelley's desk. He pushed a lock of hair from his eyes—it immediately fell back again—and studied the well-worn carpet beneath his brown suede shoes as if the faded pattern on it held some mysterious meaning.

Shelley made a sketchy introduction. 'Mr. Allard, Emery Slade, teacher of art. Emery, Mr. Craig Allard, the headmistress's son.'

Emery raised his head sufficiently to give a strained, insincere smile.

'We have met,' Craig said curtly. 'Miss Jenner?' Shelley looked up at Craig with the bold smile of someone shielded from censure. 'Let me know when my mother is available.'

'Certainly, Mr. Allard,' she replied, all honey and perfect secretary.

He gave her a cutting look, transferred it to the drooping head of her companion and went out.

'There was no need to introduce us,' said Emery. 'I've seen him around the place before. He's been away, hasn't he?'

Shelley nodded. 'Abroad for six months. He apparently left England the day I was interviewed for this job. I never met him until yesterday.'

'From his look, I'd say he'd taken to you like a duck to an oil slick—to be avoided at all costs!'

'The compliment's returned,' said Shelley sharply. 'The man's poison as far as I'm concerned. And like all poisons, I wish he'd stay out of reach.' She looked anxiously at her watch. 'Did you want something, Emery?'

He eased himself off the desk. 'Only to ask if I can call and see you this evening. I've got the urge to paint and there are too many people around this place, which is bad for my artistic health.'

Why not? Shelley asked herself. Janine would be going out with Craig. Having agreed on the time of his arrival, Emery wandered out. When Muriel Allard returned to her desk, Shelley gave her Craig's message, but she said she had already spoken to him. Then she read the letters Shelley had placed in front of her and handed them back. 'Answer them for me, dear, will you? I haven't the time.'

A little exasperatedly, Shelley nodded. Craig Allard would hardly have approved of his mother's action and Shelley herself was feeling the faintest stirrings of resentment. Not only was she expected to act as deputy head but also as the headmistress herself.

But, she argued, trying to quieten her ruffled feelings, it wasn't difficult writing tactful replies to anxious parents. Mrs. Allard had been so good to her and was such a reasonable employer, she could not now stand on her rights and say she was there to obey orders, not to give them.

Muriel Allard took out her compact and touched her nose with powder. 'I'm off, dear. The Ladies' Guild in the village have asked me to an informal coffee morning.'

If it wasn't the Ladies' Guild, Shelley thought, it would have been the vicar's wife. There was always someone, it seemed, prepared to invite Mrs. Allard into their homes and inveigle her away from her work. And Mrs. Allard was constantly willing to be so inveigled.

Janine was excited about her date with Craig Allard. She dressed with care, putting aside her patched jeans and wearing instead a floral dress with a scooped-out neckline. She pulled on long black boots.

'Where are you going?' Shelley asked, trying not to let her anxiety show.

Janine glanced out of the window into the darkness and watched the headlamps of a car approaching along the drive, throwing light in front of it like two enormous torches. 'Here's Craig,' she said. 'Ask him.'

Janine let him in. Shelley, who never bothered to dress up even when she went out with Emery, lifted a face empty of make-up and expression and asked, 'Where are you taking my sister, Mr. Allard?'

His eyes raked her and the contempt in his face told her the opinion he had formed as a result of his survey. 'Janine's over age, Miss Jenner. I can take her where I like.'

Shelley's fingers curled at her sides. 'Where are you taking her?' she repeated.

He leaned sideways against the wall. 'Shall we tell her, Janine? Put your sister out of her misery? Or shall we let her squirm with worry all the evening?'

Janine laughed gaily. 'Shelley wouldn't let worry about me spoil her evening. She keeps saying she's got no feelings left, so how can she worry?'

The eyes had not lost their contempt. 'I'm taking her to a pub, Miss Jenner. I'm going to get her drunk, then I'm going to take her on to the moors in the darkness and rape her. There now,' he straightened, 'that should keep your mind healthily occupied for the long, lonely evening.' He smiled, without warmth, at Shelley's pale face.

'She won't be lonely, Craig,' Janine said. 'Emery's coming.'

His eyes flickered. 'Is he? Have your own back, Janine, and ask your big sister what she's going to be up to while you're out with me. Is it safe, do you think,' he flung a careless arm round Janine's shoulders, 'to leave her alone with that curiously effete, ragged sort of creature who wandered into my mother's room this morning and sat on your sister's desk?'

'Safe?' said Janine, laughing. 'It's safe to leave Shelley with any man these days. Even if Emery tried anything on with her, she'd slap him down fast. She's vowed not to let another man touch her as long as she lives.'

The pale cheeks which were lifted so defiantly to Craig became flooded with colour. When would Janine stop giving away her secrets to this monster of a man?

'The touch barrier,' the guest mused, 'intriguing thought. Even the sound barrier has been smashed, Miss Jenner, so beware. Barriers were only ever put up to be broken down.'

Shelley was at her desk one morning when she heard the sound of muffled crying. It puzzled her because the children should at this time have been gathered in the hall for morning assembly.

The door creaked on its hinges and a small boy sitting on the stairs raised a tear-stained face, drawing in his breath on a convulsive sob. Shelley joined him on the bottom step, putting her arm round him. This was the boy she had found so many times sobbing in a corner, hiding his loneliness from the others. He was a withdrawn and solitary child, who did not seem to mix easily with his own kind.

Shelley often silently condemned his parents for allowing so young and sensitive a child to stay as a boarder at the school. He was not yet seven and needed the security of his home and parents. No doubt they argued, she reflected, looking at the abject little figure beside her, that by tearing him away from their constant company they were helping him to stand on his own feet. Their drastic cure for his shyness seemed to be having the opposite effect.

Shelley's usual remedy was to take the boy to her desk and produce a sweet. This normally satisfied him, although even then it would often take some time to persuade him to leave her and return to his class.

This morning Shelley pulled him close. 'Jamie,' she said, 'what's wrong? Tell Shelley.'

He rubbed his head against her arm. 'My mummy,' he said, 'I want my mummy.'

'But you're a big boy, Jamie—nearly seven. Big boys can manage without their mummies.'

But not Jamie. It seemed he found in Shelley's arms a substitute for the mother he craved and he abandoned himself to his misery. The phone rang on Mrs. Allard's desk, but Shelley ignored it. Whoever it was could call back later. At last the ringing stopped, but not Jamie's tears. There seemed to be no end to them.

There was the sound of footsteps descending the stairs, one long flight after another. Shelley knew that when those footsteps came nearer, she would have to move Jamie out of the way. But the footsteps stopped just behind them.

'Now I know,' said the owner of the two highly polished shoes not far from Shelley's head, 'why the phone wasn't answered. Mother's help, Miss Jenner, as well as deputy head and substitute teacher, not to mention your real job of personal secretary to the headmistress?'

Craig stepped past and stood in the hall looking at them. Shelley said fiercely, '*You* may be able to ignore a human being in distress, Mr. Allard, but I can't.'

'No feelings left inside you, I believe you said, Miss Jenner?' he murmured silkily. 'No male of the species was going to be allowed near you any more. What are you comforting so lovingly, so touchingly, if not a specimen of manhood, young, very young, though he may be?'

Jamie had stopped crying and appeared to be listening, although he had not moved from his comfortable position against Shelley.

'Jamie?' Shelley looked into his face. 'A sweetie, love?' He nodded and walked with her into the office, his hand clinging to hers. Craig followed, watching while the sweet was handed over and the tear-stained face dried with a paper tissue.

'Surely,' Craig asked, a touch of hardness in his voice, 'this is a job for the matron?'

Shelley glanced at Jamie, then in answer to the question chose her words with care, words which she hoped the child would not understand. 'Matron is not exactly renowned for her lightness of touch in cases of this kind, or for handing out sympathy like chocolates from a fancy box.'

She glanced anxiously at the little boy. No, he had not understood. Or had he? 'I hate Matron,' he mumbled, round the obstacle of his sweet and pressed closer to Shelley.

'All the same,' Craig persisted, 'it's what the woman's paid for. And you're paid to type letters, not to act as a wet-nurse to homesick kids.'

Shelley straightened her shoulders. 'Look, Mr. Allard, if you'd——' she took a breath, 'if you'd ever been hurt, deeply, immeasurably, irreparably hurt as I have,' another steadying breath, 'although I doubt if it's possible for any ordinary human emotion to penetrate your inflexible exterior,' she ignored the tightening of his lips, 'you'd know how it felt to be lost and—and abandoned and out of reach of comforting arms—the *right* comforting arms. Matron, with her brusqueness, would only have made matters worse, so it's surely only common humanity if I do my inadequate best rather than allow the "right" person to do her worst?'

But it seemed she had not convinced him. 'So now you're taking upon yourself the welfare of the pupils as well as the administration of the school?' He rounded on her, taking her by surprise. 'Who the blazes do you think you are?' he asked savagely. 'Are you under the illusion that you can run this place single-handed?'

Shocked by the ferocity of his attack, she cried, 'Will you stop baiting me?' Her lip quivered and she felt the small hand cling even more tightly. The significance of that grip make her blurt out, 'Don't you realise we're being overheard, every single miserable word we fling at each other is being registered on a small tape recorder of a brain? Don't you realise the effect our quarrelling must be having on the third person in this room? To his sense of security which is already threatened to the point of extinction by his separation from his parents?'

Craig looked at her curiously and there was silence for a full half minute. Then he moved, gently drawing away the little boy and putting him aside. His hands lifted and removed the glasses which framed Shelley's eyes. His fingers found their way to her armpits, gripping her firmly. His mouth descended slowly, tormentingly, to settle on hers, forcing back her head.

The pressure of his lips was hard, uncompromising and punishing, and to the girl at the receiving end of the kiss, it lasted an infinity of time. An involuntary reassuring sigh escaped from the small onlooker and Craig lifted his head, although his hands remained where they were.

His glittering, cynical eyes mocked Shelley's and he said, 'There now, Miss Jenner, are you better pleased with our relationship? You think it has made our audience a little happier to think we're friends instead of enemies? That we like instead of hate each other? And that he'll go to his class now a secure, reassured little boy and forget for a while the pain and loneliness of homesickness?'

Shelley could not answer, nor even nod. The kiss she had just been given had shattered her composure to such an extent that she wanted to find the nearest mouse-hole in the wainscoting and crawl into it, never to emerge again.

'Go to your class, lad,' Craig said gently, turning his head and smiling. Jamie nodded eagerly and ran off.

'So,' said Craig, removing his hands at last, 'in one action I've achieved two things. I've discovered within myself a reservoir—small but significant—of the milk of human kindness which I never even guessed was there. And last but certainly not least, I've stormed the outer wall of that impregnable castle my mother asserts you've built around yourself.' He glanced at his watch. 'No small achievement for such an early hour.'

As he reached the door, Shelley said dully, replacing her spectacles, 'I'm—I'm sorry for losing my temper.'

He smiled. 'You must do it again some time. I enjoyed quelling it.' In a mocking whisper, 'The pleasure was all mine.'

CHAPTER THREE

RARELY an evening went by when Craig did not take Janine out. Her face reflected the happiness she was plainly feeling. Whether it was that she was flattered by the attention of a man a good deal older than herself, whether it was infatuation, or whether—and Shelley shrank from the thought—it was genuine love that made her sister walk about in a daze in the daytime and dash out in the evening at the first sound of wheel crunching on gravel, Shelley did not know.

But she did know for certain that one day, soon, she would have to tackle either Janine, or Craig, or both.

Emery came often to the lodge, too, contriving neatly to miss Craig, who he frankly admitted he did not care to face. But Shelley had no doubt that Janine told Craig of Emery's visits. Let her tell him, she thought defiantly, and let him make what he likes of it. The kiss he had given her, intended though it was—so Craig had said—to put Jamie's mind at rest, had humiliated her beyond words.

Her only means of retaliation had been to cut Craig dead whenever they met, and if she did have to speak to him, she would do so as sharply and as briefly as possible. That her attitude did not please him she was fully aware by the animosity in his expression, but it made no difference to her behaviour.

Emery was patient about Shelley's lack of feeling where he, or any man, was concerned. He had heard of the unfortunate episode of the runaway fiancé, and had said that the man must have been crazy. With her fetching contours, which she stupidly concealed under shapeless clothes, any man who could see straight and walk straight would be drawn to her like the pointer of a compass towards the North Pole.

All he asked, he said, was to be allowed to kiss her now and then—just to prove she was female—and this she con-

35

descended to allow him to do, although he did comment, on one occasion when he said goodnight, that it was rather like kissing an item which had just been taken out of the deep freeze.

Craig continued to take Janine out. Shelley worried about their friendship. How deeply was Janine becoming involved? Even she, Shelley, prejudiced as she was against men, had to admit that there was an attraction about the man which, if she did not reinforce her barriers every time he came within sight, she herself would find difficult to resist.

He was handsome, he was worldly, his self-assurance amounted to arrogance. He dressed well, even in his relaxed moments, and the car he ran put him into the higher income bracket. How could a girl as impressionable as Janine resist such a combination of charms?

One morning Craig came into the headmistress's office. Mrs. Allard had gone to Middlesbrough to look at some secondhand educational equipment.

Craig's manner was cool. As she looked at him looking down at her, she experienced a thought so treacherous it filled her with dismay. If only, the thought said, he would look at me once, just once, the way he looks at Janine. Instead of that derision, if there could be a momentary softening, a smile, sincere and pleasing....

She jammed on her mental brakes. What was she doing, hoping for an improvement in their relations, seeking a smile from him instead of a scowl, sympathy in place of studied cynicism? If so, she was wasting her time.

Her glasses rested on the desk top. She rammed them on and glared up at him. 'You want me?'

'No.'

The response was immediate and unequivocal, and spoken with a mocking, insulting smile. She coloured as she sensed the insinuation that in no possible circumstances could he regard her in that light. There also arose from somewhere inside her, like a deep-sea creature surfacing for the first time in years, a curious sensation of yearning.

Stunted, half-developed though it was, it was unmistakable—and terrifyingly familiar. But what frightened her

36

most was its potential strength, like a firework in a nightmare turning in mid-air into a life-destroying rocket. All the ingredients were there, she could sense it, it needed only a catalyst to cause the chemical reaction to come about. And the end result? she asked herself despairingly. An emotional upheaval which would make her relationship with Michael Townley seem like an adolescent crush.

Craig sat in the chair at his mother's desk. 'Would you come over here, please?' he asked distantly. 'Bring your chair.'

His fingers played with his mother's desk calendar. It was the kind that rotated, the new date slipping automatically into place. The continuous clicking sound it made jarred on Shelley's nerves, the fact that it would take a lot of her precious time turning it back to the correct date when he had finished fiddling with it ruffled her even more.

'I don't know whether my mother has told you,' his glance flicked her like someone trying out the timbre of a wine glass, 'but, having largely completed my research, I'm now in the process of writing a book. I—er——' *Click-click* went the calendar, 'I'm what you might call a two-fingered typist and——'

'You're asking me to help you out?'

The narrowed eyes rested on her. The calendar was replaced on the desk, now hopelessly out of date. 'How did you guess?' He leaned back, crossing his legs, his eyes still on her. 'Since you've come to the point so quickly, so shall I. Will you help me?'

For a long time Shelley did not answer. Everything within her, her thoughts, her emotions, her better judgment urged her to say 'no'.

'I'll make it worth your while.'

She glanced at him indignantly. Was that what he thought was worrying her? But still she could not bring out that simple word 'yes'.

His eyes had not left her. 'I believe you're hoping one day to finance Janine in opening a shop of her own?'

'What if I am?'

He sighed. 'I'm handling this badly.' He leaned forward, clasping his hands over the desk. 'Shelley,' the word left his lips, hitting her and setting up such a vibration in the region of her heart she could hardly stand it, 'I need your help.' He smiled and her heart lurched drunkenly. What was the matter with her? First her name, than a smile from him and she was in such an emotional turmoil she might have been a fourteen-year-old experiencing her first infatuation ...

At last she answered, and the words came out dry and husky, 'What do you want me to do?'

His eyes held hers steadily. 'I have four handwritten chapters. Some of the work is messy but most, I hope, is readable. Would you type what I've written so that I can get on with the corrections?'

Without hesitation she replied, 'Yes. But I'll do it without money.'

'Which is exactly what my mother said you would say. I discussed it with her and she agreed to let me ask you.'

'But, Mr. Allard,' Shelley said urgently, 'if you mean me to do it in school hours, I'm afraid that's not——'

'In school hours, when you're acting head, deputy head, welfare officer, secretary, comforter of weeping kids ...' He stood, pushing in the chair. 'Of course not, woman. Have some sense. In your spare time. And the money will be yours whether you want it or not. I ask no favours of the girl who dislikes me as much as you do.'

'When shall I start?' she asked tonelessly.

'This evening?' She nodded. 'Upstairs in my apartment. Time? Shall we say seven until—when? Until nine? Name your price.'

She shook her head. 'I'll leave that to you.'

'Fair enough. You'll accept whatever I choose to pay?' She nodded and he named a sum which he would pay her hourly.

'Far too much, Mr. Allard.'

'I hope, Miss Jenner, you're going to work hard and be worth every penny. Otherwise,' with a smile, 'I shall demand my money back.'

She answered seriously, 'I won't let you down.'

He smiled as he answered, 'The thought that you would had never even occurred to me. I have every confidence

38

in—and admiration for—your *professional* integrity.'

The emphasis on the penultimate word told her with painful clarity how little admiration he had for her as a woman.

'Craig's taking me out again tonight,' Janine told Shelley over tea.

Shelley said, doing her best to sound casual, 'You're not getting too involved with that man, are you, Jan?'

'If you mean am I looking for a ring from him to put on my finger, no.'

Shelley said with a gentle smile, 'You haven't really answered my question.'

Janine shrugged. 'I do like him, but—what's the use? He's way above me. I'm trying to stop myself getting serious, but it's not easy, Shelley. He's got everything, looks, money, status, brains. Me, I'm so dim I wonder he can stand me.' She laughed and brightened.

But Shelley did not laugh. 'It's not fair the way he's paying you so much attention. If he's just playing with you——'

'Oh, leave it, Shelley. If he throws me overboard, I can take it. No doubt I'll splash and flounder at first, but I won't drown. There are plenty of other men around. In the meantime, I'm taking what's offered. Like you should be with Emery.'

'I told you, Jan, I want no deep involvement with any man. I've finished with all that.'

'You've said that so many times I wonder if you're really saying it to convince yourself?'

Shelley looked up quickly. Her young sister was growing up, she was more perspicacious than she, Shelley, had given her credit for. And maybe Jan was right.

Shelley explained that Craig had asked her to help him with his book. 'I'm starting the work tonight.'

Janine said with a laugh, 'So if he's late calling for me, I'll know who's to blame!'

Craig was dressed and ready for going out when Shelley arrived. A twinge—was it of pain?—a quick twist inside her caught her unawares as she looked at him stretched out lazily on the settee. He lifted himself upright and his manner was as relaxed as his clothes.

His jacket, high-collared, was unbuttoned. A belt hung, unfastened, from loops. His shirt was white and roll-necked, his trousers well-fitting. She experienced a feeling of panic as she looked at him. The sense of being on the edge of something devastating and entirely strange welled up in her again.

'You look,' he said casually, 'as though you've just come face to face with an escaped animal from a zoo. I'm not wild, Miss Jenner. I won't tear you limb from limb. Unless,' with a grin, 'you make too many typing errors. Relax, have a drink.' He poured one from a cocktail cabinet. 'Make yourself at home. When your sister comes here she takes possession.'

'My sister's been here?' Her tone was sharp.

'Yes.' The drink was handed to her. 'Why not?' He lifted his glass ironically. 'Cheers'. He drank.

'She—she just hasn't mentioned it.' Shelley sipped her drink.

Craig's lips curved into a taunting smile. 'Now you're wondering what we do up here.'

'The thought never crossed my mind,' she bluffed.

'Come, come, Miss Jenner. And you a once-engaged, almost-married woman? You know the facts of life.'

Shelley felt cold inside. Her sister here, at night, with this man, with his attractions, his knowledge of the opposite sex, his—his pulling power—there was no other way of describing the effect he had on a woman.

The liquid left the glass and poured into her throat. Then she stood.

'I've come to work, Mr. Allard.' She took her spectacles from their case and put them on.

He drawled, 'Craig Allard put in his place. Must you wear those perishing things?' motioning with his head.

'My glasses? Yes, for work. Why?'

'They hardly enhance your looks.'

She coloured angrily. 'I have none to enhance.'

'I'm not going to disagree with that statement, even if you hoped I would. With that hairstyle, with the clothes you wear a schoolgirl wouldn't be seen dead in, with the sour, reproving manner you choose to adopt in my—and who knows, any man's—presence, who could possibly call you attractive?' He folded his arms and dwelt on the fury and humiliation in her face. 'I saw a girl once at your house —Janine's sister it was—it couldn't have been you!— dressed like a bride, soft, feminine, womanly ... kissable——'

Shelley walked to the door, but he was behind her, gripping her by the shoulders, swinging her round. 'Wrong way, Miss Jenner. The desk is over there, under the window. Typewriter's at the ready, notes crying out to be translated into legible English. Let me lead you by the hand.' This he took and grasped, despite her struggle to remove it. He pushed her down into the chair. 'Paper, carbons, my notes.'

'And,' belligerently, 'if there's anything I don't understand?'

'Mm.' He rubbed his chin. 'I'm taking Janine out.'

'I know.'

An eyebrow lifted. 'You don't approve?' She pressed her lips together. 'No, you don't. Too bad. This is between Janine and myself.'

She stood up. He forced her down. 'When will you concede that your sister's a big girl now?' He consulted his watch. 'Look, if you get stuck, leave spaces and I'll fill in when I return.' At the door he said, 'Shelley? Thanks.'

Next morning Craig phoned Shelley to ask how long she had stayed. 'Two and a half hours,' she told him.

'From the amount you accomplished I wouldn't have been surprised if you had stayed until midnight.'

'You wouldn't have known if I had, would you?'

'Are you trying to tell me,' his voice was abrasive, 'that I kept your sister out too late?' The voice softened menacingly. 'Do you know, Miss Jenner, you get under my skin so much sometimes that if you were a man I'd have knocked you flying long ago. Just take warning from that, will you?'

She slammed down the phone and hid her face in her hands.

A few days later Muriel Allard went away. 'I need a

holiday,' she told Shelley. 'I booked some time ago to go on a cruise. I didn't tell anyone, not even Craig. I thought if I did, something would be sure to crop up to stop me! You can manage without me for a fortnight, can't you? I have every confidence in you, you know.'

Shelley was silently appalled at what her employer seemed to be expecting of her. But she was determined to rise to the challenge. She had nothing else to occupy her time, only Craig's typing which filled two or three evenings every week. He never remained in his apartment while she worked. He seemed to make a point of going out, sometimes with Janine and sometimes, Shelley believed, he even went for walks. It was almost as if he could not stay in his own flat while she was in any part of it...

But that evening he was waiting for her. 'So my mother's going away yet again?' he greeted her. 'Who's doing her job in her absence?'

Shelley, who had just pushed her spectacles into place on her nose, snapped the case shut. She did not answer.

'Forgive me if I'm wrong, but is it you?'

His tone worried her. 'It's little more than I usually do, Mr. Allard. Even when your mother's here, I speak to parents on her behalf, placate when necessary, remind them gently that their fees are due, tell them when their little ones are misbehaving.'

His eyes narrowed. 'And how much is my mother paying you?' She hesitated. 'Tell me, please. I happen to be the owner of the premises, if not the school. Look upon me as the landlord, if you like, a landlord with a financial stake in the establishment. I have a right to know.'

Shelley told him. 'Slave labour,' he muttered. 'When my mother returns, I shall have a talk with her on the subject of your pay.'

'I'm not complaining.'

'Maybe you aren't. I am. Now, these notes I've made. A little more illegible than usual, unfortunately—written in the small hours. If you want me, I'll be around, if not in my flat then somewhere in the school. It's time I did a bit of checking up on this place of learning. Some of the teachers live in. I'll call on them socially, chat them up, find out if the standards are slipping.'

By the time he returned, Shelley had removed her spectacles and was preparing to leave. He swept in and motioned her to the other end of the room, putting a drink into her hand. He walked up and down, then threw himself into a chair. He was silent and something stopped Shelley from interrupting his thoughts. He was not communicating, yet he did not appear to want to be alone.

At last he said, in a tone tinged with disgust, 'To listen to some of those teachers,' he motioned outside towards the living quarters, 'you would think the technological revolution just hasn't happened.' He leaned forward and turned up the gas fire fitted into the closed-in fireplace. Then he warmed his palms against the heat. 'It's their attitude that gets me. They're up to their necks in the past, like someone sucked into a bog, and they won't use their brains as a last resort to get themselves out of it and into the twentieth century.'

Shelley watched his profile and somewhere inside her something stirred into life. She did not give herself the chance to analyse and speculate. Instead she tore her eyes away and dwelt on the hissing incandescent source of heat which shed its warmth on them both.

'I think,' he reflected, 'it's the cloistered atmosphere, the cosy, snug, insulated conditions under which they teach.' He looked at her and she felt a flick of pleasure that he remembered she was there. 'I don't like fee-paying schools. As an educationalist, I find they go against my grain.'

'And yet you gave this house to your mother so that she could open one?'

He laughed and leaned back. 'Yes, I see the irony of it. But it was a case of filial affection overcoming my personal prejudices. Which is also why I help her with the school financially. No other reason. How could it be otherwise? My professional side shrinks from the idea of an educated élite, which is what this school is helping to produce.' He closed his eyes. 'If I had my way I'd close it down.'

Shelley watched his quiet features and felt ice finger her spine. Close the school? That would mean the end of her job and make her and Janine homeless. He couldn't mean

43

it? It would be the end of—so many things...

He said reflectively, 'I can't stand kids in the mass.'

'But—but you're a teacher.'

He opened his eyes. 'Ah, yes, but I'm a teacher of teachers. A big difference.'

'So,' with an odd twinge of disappointment, 'you don't like children.'

'Other people's children, not particularly. My own? Well,' with a twinkle, 'to my knowledge I haven't any.'

She coloured and leaned back in the chair. And if he had, if he'd been around, gathering experience in other women's arms, what did it matter to her? *It did!* The realisation came like an incendiary device hitting the ground at her feet and enveloping her in flame. No reason could put out the fire, no attempt to rationalise could stop the truth burning up her heart.

'Tell me,' his half-closed eyes surveyed her, 'you're an intelligent woman—a contradiction in terms, of course; it isn't possible to be both intelligent and a woman——' He watched her colour deepen and the angry words move her lips then he held up his hand. 'All right, I only said it to provoke. I enjoy teasing you. You look so much more attractive when there's red in your cheeks and your eyes try to burn me up. Much less of the schoolmarm and much more of the beautiful creature you are underneath all that surliness and hate.' Again she flushed, this time with a strange mixture of embarrassment and pleasure. But although his eyes lingered on her face a moment longer, he said, 'Do *you* think it's wrong for a small, select section of the population to be able to send their children to a school like this one?'

'If they choose to do so and can afford it——'

'Ah, yes, freedom of choice, all part of that democracy we pride ourselves on so much. But the children here are cocooned in a benign environment with the only disturbance ruffling their calm waters being in the shape of a dragon of a housemother—or matron, call her what you will. They hate her to a man, or rather, boy.'

'But surely a school like this has the money to buy the best equipment?' Shelley ventured.

'Perhaps, but you've got to get the services of teachers

who are trained to use such equipment. Either my mother has chosen her staff wrongly, too subjectively—say, a liking for their looks, their manners, their accents—instead of objectively, on the basis of their qualifications and their past experience, or such people don't exist. I suspect the former—my mother's damned intuition which she exercises and relies on as a substitute for down-to-earth knowledge.' He eyed her. 'Isn't that how she chose you? Intuition? Had a feeling, she told me naïvely, that you'd be right for the job.'

'Well,' defiantly, 'was she wrong?'

'Right in one way. That you were so unselfish and self-sacrificing you'd recognise no limits to your function as a mere secretary. That where your heart called so you would follow, and be damned to your terms of reference as a secretarial assistant. If a nurse was needed, you'd be there. If a tame psychologist was called for, you'd be that psychologist. I'm referring to that homesick little boy. If an uncertificated teacher was required as a fill-in, you'd act the part. If a substitute head teacher—at a poorly paid secretary's pay—you'd be that substitute. Yes, she chose well and wisely from her own point of view.'

'But not,' fiercely, 'the children's?'

'The children's?' with a shrug. 'If it's comfort they need, a bit of plaster slapped on a grazed knee, a soft and shapely bosom to nuzzle against in time of stress, perhaps. But from the point of view of real knowledge, of academic achievement (which, after all, is what their parents are paying for), or accomplished nursing care, no, not the children's.'

Her lips were tight, her cheeks pale. She stood up. 'You want me to resign from my job?'

He drew himself lazily from the chair. 'Resign? Good heavens, no. If you went, my mother would have to employ at least six other people in your place. If it pleases you to act so many roles at such shockingly low pay, carry on. If it gives you the feeling that there's a halo somewhere around here,' his hand stroked her hair and his fingers trailed down her cheek, 'and it makes you feel wanted—don't we all at times?—then carry on, Miss Jenner, carry on. Who am I to stop you from carrying out your good works? Think of the money you're saving the family!'

Shelley walked stiffly to the door. Her cheeks still tingled from the touch of his fingers. 'Goodnight, Mr. Allard.'

'Goodnight, Miss Jenner. Come again tomorrow?' She was breathing so hard as a result of his cynical summing-up of her unselfish actions, she did not answer. 'Don't worry,' he murmured, with a taunting smile, 'I shall be out.'

'In that case, Mr. Allard, yes, I shall come again tomorrow.' If she had hoped to crush him, she had badly miscalculated. He laughed out loud as he watched her move swiftly from the room.

CHAPTER FOUR

So much work accumulated as a result of Mrs. Allard's absence, Shelley found herself working increasingly later into the evening. Sometimes, after typing for Craig, she would return to her desk in the office and tackle many of the items she had not been able to deal with during the day.

Shelley had told Craig none of this, and he did not look at her long enough to realise how much her tiredness showed. They rarely met, anyway. Even when she went to his apartment to type for him, he had usually gone before she arrived.

Emery was patience itself. For an artist, his temperament was surprisingly equable. Had it been otherwise, Shelley reflected, he would either have exploded into an artistic tantrum at her constant preoccupation with work out of hours, or found someone else. He did neither. He simply painted and sketched, and when he had finished, he painted and sketched again.

One evening Shelley arrived home during the evening to find Janine sitting over the fire—it was necessary to have one alight although it was early April—and looking sorry for herself.

'Boy-friend let you down?' Shelley asked with a touch of sarcasm.

'If you mean Craig,' Janine responded in a tone so depressed Shelley became concerned, 'yes. He rang to say he had a business engagement this evening and couldn't come. So I went for a walk. And guess who I saw driving along with a beautiful woman at his side? Craig Allard.'

'And who,' asked Shelley, her heart beating painfully hard, 'was the woman?'

'Sylva Wallasey-Browne. Who else?'

The anger that made her fingers curl, Shelley told herself, was on her sister's behalf, no one else's. 'Isn't there a rumour that he was once her boy-friend?'

Janine nodded. 'I could cry. Why wasn't he honest? Why didn't he say he didn't want my company any more and was brushing me off?'

The phone rang. Shelley answered. 'Can I speak to Janine, please?' the voice asked.

'Is that Mr. Allard?'

'It is. And am I speaking to the redoubtable Miss Shelley Jenner?'

'My sister's very upset, Mr. Allard.'

'Oh?' The mocking note had disappeared. 'May I ask why?'

'Because,' Shelley rushed on, against her better judgment which was urging her to stop, 'you lied to her. A business engagement, you said. Since when has another woman been a business engagement?'

'Your sister, Miss Jenner,' there was brittle anger in his tone, 'can be as upset as she likes. I'm under no obligation to her in any shape or form. There are no ties between us, no promises have been exchanged. We merely go around together. Is that understood?' The receiver crashed down.

'Shelley!' Janine shrieked. 'Let me speak to him. You had no right——'

'He's gone,' Shelley said dully.

She left Janine madly dialling Craig's number. 'Craig,' she heard, 'don't take any notice of Shelley. I've told you before, she hates men, especially you. I don't, Craig, you know that...'

Next morning, Craig was in his mother's room when Shelley went in. He was leafing through documents on the desk but pushed them aside when she entered. His mood was bad, Shelley judged, by the way he looked at her.

'I'd like to clear the air between us, Miss Jenner, in relation to our acid conversation on the phone last night. First, who saw me with the so-called "other woman"?' Shelley told him. 'Janine. Right. Secondly, even if Sylva Wallasey-Browne were a girl-friend of mine, that would be my business and no one else's. Despite the fact that I take your sister out, I'm a free agent where women are concerned. Is that clear?'

Shelley dropped her belongings on her desk across the room. 'But—but where does my sister fit into your picture? You can't get a girl fond of you—and I can see with my own eyes that she is—and shrug it off as if it were of no importance.'

He strolled towards her, eyes slitted. 'Are you asking me my intentions?'

Shelley's head drooped and she sank on to her chair utterly at a loss as to how to deal with the situation—or the man.

'Let's get this straight. I have no "intentions" regarding your sister.'

Her head lifted. 'So what are you doing? Playing around with her, breaking her heart? I've suffered that way, remember, and I don't want it to happen to her. You're not going to hurt her as another man hurt me. Stop misleading her——'

'And you stop seeing your sister through rose-tinted spectacles. She's no more serious than I am about our relationship. She's just immensely flattered.'

'You're wrong, I'm sure you're wrong. When she saw you last night with that—with Sylva Wallasey-Browne she was terribly upset.'

'No doubt she was, at being deprived of an expensive meal at one of the many restaurants and hotels I take her to.'

Shelley felt she should let the subject rest, but something drove her on. 'My—my sister hasn't any depth, Mr. Allard. She's sweet and pretty, and fundamentally a happy person, but she's not your intellectual equal. If you—if you married her eventually, it would founder.'

Why, she asked herself, was she persisting like this? What was she hoping to get from this conversation?

'I haven't got marriage in mind, Miss Jenner, not where any woman is concerned. I have no wish—no need—to tie myself down.' His anger left him and he lounged against her desk, hands deep in his pockets. The expression on his face warned of the baiting to come. 'I need women only for relaxation, and by that I mean physical relaxation. I don't need them to relax my mind. I could find that outlet in reading novels or watching films.'

Shelley's heart began slowly, inexorably, to sink. She knew now for what she had been searching in pressing the subject.

'Nor,' Craig went on relentlessly, 'do I need women to stimulate my mind. My work obliges in that respect. Therefore I don't "need" intelligent women. In fact,' he looked her over, her glasses now in position, 'I shy away from them. The more intelligent a woman is, the more I keep her at arms' length. So don't worry about your sister at my hands. I find her amusing and a diversion, nothing more.'

Her drawn-in lips, her suppressed anger moved him to a mocking smile. 'And,' he went on, 'when sex "rears its ugly head", as the saying goes, your sister is perfectly capable of making up her own mind about how far she goes or allows me to go.' Shelley winced. 'She's no child. You may have watched over her for years, from puberty to young womanhood, but she doesn't need you clucking round her like a frustrated old hen any more.'

Now Shelley's lips quivered and she stood to face him. 'How *can* you speak to me like that? After all I've done for her, looking after her when our parents died, working overtime to earn more money so that she could be apprenticed to a hairdresser. Even,' her voice lowered, 'to sacrificing my marriage.' Craig's eyebrows rose. 'In the end my—my fiancé threatened to refuse to have Jan living with us after we were married.' Shelley looked away. 'The night before our wedding we quarrelled—over Jan. Then Michael said he couldn't go through with it. Needless to say, I didn't tell Jan the whole story.'

He looked at her steadily. 'So it's not true that he found someone else?'

'Yes, it is true. He—he said he didn't love me any more, and he was sorry it had taken him until the eve of our wedding to find it out. Now,' she challenged him, 'do you see why I don't trust any man?'

He lifted his shoulders. 'I can't blame you. If I'd been in your position and a woman did that to me, I wouldn't trust any woman.'

With that he left her.

Shelley worked late again that evening. Immediately after her evening meal she returned to the office and took her place at Mrs. Allard's desk. Emery had brought some work with him which kept him occupied for some time. Then he walked across the room and lifted Shelley's hair which was in its usual 'tail'.

'Undo this for me, Shelley.' She looked up, startled. 'I want to sketch you sitting at that great big desk acting the great big executive.'

Reluctantly she released her hair and it swung round her face, softening her features. Emery removed her glasses. 'That's better. Now carry on working.' He switched on the light and returned to his seat. 'Forget I'm here.'

So, with the greatest of ease, Shelley forgot Emery was there. There were a number of puzzling items in Mrs. Allard's post and she wished she could ring her employer on the ship on which she was cruising—through the Mediterranean, wasn't it?—and ask her advice.

When Emery had finished he showed Shelley the sketch of herself. She asked if she could keep it, but he refused. 'I haven't got much of you, heaven knows. So I'm keeping this. Sorry.' He bent down and kissed her upturned mouth, once, twice.

The door opened. Craig Allard watched as the kiss ended hurriedly. He contemplated the red faces and the confusion. With agitated hands Shelley lifted her hair from her face, but it sprang back over her cheeks.

'Ter-rouble,' Emery murmured, rolling the word round his tongue.

'Yes, Mr. Allard?' Shelley asked faintly.

Craig answered curtly, 'I saw the light in my mother's office, so I came to investigate.' He looked at Emery, who took the hint the look contained.

'I,' Emery said philosophically, 'know how and when to make myself scarce, but fast. 'Bye, Shelley. See you,' he raised his hand, shot a glance at Craig and said to Shelley, 'all in one piece, I hope,' took his belongings with him and left Shelley to her fate.

'So,' said Craig, his eyes subjecting her hairstyle and her

casual clothes to a close scrutiny, 'for your boy-friend you become a woman.'

Under his estimating gaze her fingers and toes curled. She was painfully conscious of the old striped shirt she had pulled on, which stretched tightly across her breasts, a size too small because it had belonged to Janine; the belted, faded denim pants she had picked up from the floor of her wardrobe.

Since she was not officially on duty, she had decided that anything would do in the way of dress, but Craig's hard eyes were merciless, making the most of her slightly dishevelled appearance. Shelley found herself move involuntarily in a squirming, twisting motion.

'If you must make love,' he drawled, 'I'd be obliged if you would do it on your own premises and not in my mother's office, at my mother's desk.'

'You've got it all wrong, Mr. Allard,' Shelley protested, wishing for some inexplicable reason to set the record straight.

But he snapped, 'I believe what I see. In any case,' he looked at his watch, 'what are you doing here? Your office hours end at five.'

'Officially, they do, but when your mother's away, there's so much to do I can't get it all done in the day. So when I'm not typing for you, I come back here in the evenings.'

'To do what, for heaven's sake?'

'The admin work.'

'*You*, tackle the administration of the school in my mother's absence?'

'Who else is there?' There was a touch of appeal in her voice. 'No one knows as much about it as I do.'

He gave an exasperated sigh and came to stand beside her. She felt his approach as if it were a physical thing. What made her so aware of this man? Why did one part of her want to pull away and the other, in her imagination, reach out towards him?

Now the feel of him—although no part of him touched her—was unbearable. She tried in desperation to separate her reason from her emotions and failed miserably. They were as one in their desire—to make contact with this man beside her.

Then he bent down, one hand on the back of her chair, the other with the palm flat against the desk top. He was so close his jacket brushed her arm, his chest pressed against her shoulder. She wanted to turn, reach up and pull his head down, to feel his cheek against hers . . .

She reined in her thoughts, pushing her hair back with a shaking hand. Her eyes sought his, hoping he had not guessed at the tumult that was whipping her emotions into a state of near-hysteria. She met a cool, mocking smile. He knew, she was convinced, just what he was doing to her!

'Show me,' he said, 'an example of the kind of work you're tackling.'

Glad of a diversion, she sorted with flustered fingers through the pile of papers she had been studying. 'These are the applications for the post of deputy head. I've been sorting through them——'

Instead of pleasing him, her words made him angry. 'You're hardly qualified to tell the good from the bad. Don't tell me you were attempting to draw up a short list?'

Her eyes were tearful as they sought his. Why could she never please him? 'Who else is there to do it, Mr. Allard? And these,' she extracted a handful of forms, 'for a mathematics teacher.'

He straightened. 'Get up, woman. Let me sit down. This is going to be a long job.' He motioned to the phone. 'Get your sister for me. I had a date with her.'

Janine answered brightly. Shelley thought, with a touch of compassion, 'She's going to be disappointed.'

Craig took the phone and Shelley could tell by the sound of Janine's voice just how disappointed she was. 'What's keeping you?' she wailed.

He glanced with a hint of spite at Shelley. 'It's not a case of what, sweetie, but who. Another woman, that's who's keeping me. In fact, she's sitting on my knee with her arms round my neck.' There was an even louder wail from the other end, and Craig laughed. 'It's your sister who's come between us. There now, you should be writhing with jealousy! You are? Then you can quit worrying right now. It's work, pure and simple, that's the cause of the trouble. Your sister doesn't lavish her feminine charms, if she has any,' his glance swivelled sideways and lifted, but no higher than the portion of Shelley's anatomy which strained against her shirt, 'on me. Tomorrow evening? Doubt it, I'm writing a book, as if you didn't know. I'll ring you at the shop if I can make it.' He rang off.

'Pull up a chair,' he said shortly, 'and stay quiet while I read, learn and digest.'

'But, Mr. Allard, I've studied most of it in detail. Perhaps I could——'

'When I want your assistance, I'll tell you.' He contemplated the mixture of frustration and anger on her face, then transferred his eyes to the pile of papers.

Some minutes later, during which time Shelley had chafed and fidgeted, he surfaced. 'Got your notepad? Right, take these names and head the list "Candidates recommended for consideration for the short list for the post of deputy head teacher." ' He then dictated six names, and passed on to the vacancies for teachers. Then he flicked through the remaining pile of papers.

'There's something amongst those I can't quite understand, Mr. Allard,' Shelley ventured.

'You don't say,' he commented dryly. 'Someone trained in office practice should surely be equal to the administration of a privately run boarding and day school?' His smile was quizzical and she coloured.

'It's connected with a proposed extension to the school,' she told him. 'Your mother seems to be putting the work out for tender, but I can't trace anywhere that she's applied for planning permission. I would have thought that was essential before getting builders' estimates.'

'You're right, Miss Jenner. Trust my mother to overlook such an important fact. I'm fond of her, but that doesn't prevent me from criticising her. To be frank, I think she took on this school on a wave of enthusiasm.' He leaned back to talk to her. 'You know, the realisation of a life-long dream, and now she's seen just how dedicated and hardworking you have to be to run such a place, so that it develops and doesn't stagnate, she's up and away and trying to put the whole project out of her mind.'

He turned his attention to the plans of the proposed extension and tapped the papers with his finger. 'This was the "business" I had to see the Wallasey-Brownes about, although your sister didn't believe me. Sylva's parents had offered to invest money in the school if these extensions were built. But their economic circumstances have changed and they've withdrawn their offer. Since my mother was away on one of her interminable trips abroad, they invited me there to break the news. After which I took Sylva for a drink, just to show there was no ill feeling. So tell your little sister that, will you? She still doesn't believe it could have been "business" that made me break our date when she saw the beautiful Sylva in my car.' He gave her a crooked smile. 'Do *you* believe me?'

'Implicitly. But does it matter?'

He examined her face for a few moments, then turned away, saying indifferently, 'Not really. While I look through this lot, could you produce some coffee from somewhere?'

Shelley nodded and went through to the kitchens, asking Mrs. Allard's housekeeper for a tray of coffee and biscuits. When it was ready, Shelley carried it into the office.

Craig looked up. 'What did you do, wave a magic wand?' Shelley explained and he commented, leaning back and relaxing, 'Resourceful, aren't you? Intelligent, too.' He watched while she poured.

'Which, of course, doesn't commend me to you.'

He looked up at her as she handed him his coffee. 'To use the words you flung at me a few minutes ago, does it matter?'

She inched the chair from his side and, satisfied at last with the distance she had put between them, drank her coffee. He watched her activities with a quizzical interest. 'It doesn't matter to me in the least, Mr. Allard, whether you like me or not.'

She expected retaliation and sure enough, it came. With lowered lids he did a detailed survey of her outline, just as Emery, if he had been sketching her, would have done. Craig said, 'You're a shapely wench, aren't you? I wonder that any man could be enticed away from you once you'd got your claws into him. Tell me,' he hitched an arm over the back of the chair, 'how would you set about keeping a man from straying if you really wanted him? Would you offer him certain—inducements, or would you just let him walk away without a fight?'

'Fight? I wouldn't bother myself. No man is worth fighting for.' Even as she spoke the words she knew they were not true. This man, who seemed to take such pleasure in tormenting her—he would be worth fighting for.

'Bitter,' he commented, 'acrimonious, even after—how long?'

'Since I broke with Michael? Seven months.'

'Mm. From the look of you your external injuries have healed, but internally you're still bleeding. Any chance of a reconciliation with the man?'

'None at all. I told you he found someone else.'

'If he ever came back to you, would you take him?' The question caught her unawares.

'I—I really don't know. Perhaps. It—it would depend on so many things.'

But deep in her heart she knew that Michael was part of her past. He had no place in her future.

'Do you intend to spend the rest of your life moping for him?'

'No,' she answered shortly. 'I've put him out of my mind. All the same, I'm not allowing any man to get near me again, either mentally or——' She eyed him uncomfortably, leaving the sentence unfinished.

But he finished it for her. He stood, put out a hand and caught hers. He tugged her from the chair and pulled her hard against him. 'Physically?' Her body, where it touched his, caught fire. 'You know,' he said softly, 'you shouldn't say a thing like that to a man. It challenges him and when a woman—an attractive woman—challenges a man, there's no knowing what will happen next.'

It was imperative that she should escape from him, so she jerked her body petulantly. He let her go and she could not quell the quicksilver tingle of disappointment which ran up her spine.

But he had not finished with her. She had moved to the

other side of the desk, but he strolled round it to face her again. 'You're—how old?—twenty-five? Let me give you some advice. Do you know the poem by Edmund Waller, *Go, Lovely Rose?* He asks the rose to give a message to his lady-love. Take note of the last two verses, Miss Jenner.' Softly he quoted, '*Small is the worth of beauty from the light retired; Bid her come forth, Suffer herself to be desired, And not blush so to be admired, Then die—that she the common fate of all things rare may read in thee; How small a part of time they share That are so wondrous sweet and fair!*'

She ran to the door and put it between them.

Muriel Allard returned from her cruise. While Shelley was busy elsewhere, the headmistress had a long session with her son. When he had gone and Shelley took her place at her desk again, she found her employer agitated and flushed. This was so much out of character that Shelley asked if she was well.

'Perfectly, dear.' Muriel added disarmingly, 'I've had something of a reprimand from my son, a kind of mental rap over the knuckles. Absenting myself from duty and so on. But,' she shook her head like a bewildered child, 'I can't help being something of a nomad. It's in my blood. I crave for a change of scene if I'm too long in one place. I told him I had every confidence in you as my secretary to cope in my absence. He said you had not only acted as my ultra-efficient secretary, but as the whole darned administration! Is that true, dear?'

'Well, I——' Confused, not liking to admit the truth, Shelley shrugged. 'As you said,' she finished feebly, 'I coped.' She did not add, 'With your son's help.' It seemed as though Craig had not told his mother of his timely intervention into the affairs of the school.

'I can't promise I won't go off again, that's the trouble,' Mrs. Allard said, with a pleading look in her eyes. She laughed, regaining her sense of humour. 'It's a kind of affliction I have. Perhaps I could take some medicine for it!'

But Shelley knew there would be no cure for Mrs.

Allard's wanderlust. She also knew, deep down, that Mapleleaf House School could not function indefinitely with an increasingly absent headmistress. The threat to her and Janine's existence, happiness and security was so great that she did not dare to contemplate the consequences of Mrs. Allard's constant craving for a change of scene.

'You know,' she told her employer, with some trepidation, 'that the annual parents' day is fixed for a month's time.'

'I have to admit, dear,' with a smile, 'that I've been doing my best to forget the fact. But the information is here,' she patted her head, 'filed away. I doubt if you'll allow it to gather dust!' She frowned, a little worried. 'My son tells me I'm not only working you too hard, I'm also underpaying you.'

'Please,' Shelley rushed in, 'don't worry about my salary. *I* haven't complained. I'm content, I'm not asking for more.'

Mrs. Allard sighed. 'Then that's all right. You see, the finances of the school are not as stable as they might be. What with price increases in every line ... my son is pressing me to increase the fees, but I'm afraid to do so in case the parents simply could not meet them and take their children away.'

She gave another breathy sigh, put her doubts behind her and got down to work.

It was a Saturday morning in the Easter holidays. The school was deserted, except for the boarders whose parents lived and worked abroad. One or two teachers who lived at the school organised outings to keep the boys from fretting too much.

Shelley was in the kitchen washing the breakfast dishes. Emery had gone home to Lancashire and Janine was at work at Mrs. Caversham's hairdressing salon in the village. The front door was pushed open and Craig strolled in. He watched Shelley from the doorway.

'A testimonial for you,' he commented without a preliminary greeting, 'would run oddly. I quote, "Not only is Miss Jenner able to run a private educational establishment

58

singlehanded, but she's domesticated into the bargain. Intelligent, when she cares to exercise her brain, decorative when she likes to make the effort. The only thing she lacks is a heart, warmth, responsiveness—everything that makes a man want to grab her and say, "She belongs to me. Hands off." '

She faced him, pressing back against the sink. 'If that's all you've come for, to laugh at me, then you can just turn round and leave the way you came.'

He had only been in the room a few moments and yet her heart was pounding as if she had run uphill carrying a loaded furniture van. It was that odd feeling he provoked in her of wanting to hit back at him every time he came within talking distance. Michael had never affected her in such a way. If he had, would he now be married to her instead of being the boy-friend of another woman?

Craig strolled across to face her, arms folded, legs slightly apart. 'Thanks for the charming welcome, which is what I've come to expect from you. Nevertheless, I refuse to take umbrage. Instead, I'm going to give you an order. Dry your dripping hands, leave those perishing dishes and go and collect your swimming outfit. A spade and pail, too, if you like. You're going out.'

'I'm sorry, thanks for the thought, but I can't. Janine's coming home for lunch.'

He moved a little nearer, crowding her in against the cupboard beneath the stainless steel sink unit. As she pressed closer to it, so he moved again until their bodies made contact. 'I'm taking you,' he said, ignoring her burning cheeks and strangled breathing, 'to the coast, to Runswick Bay. Now run along like a good girl and get your things.'

She shook her head, disturbed beyond words at his nearness. 'I told you, Mr. Allard, I can't. It's impossible.'

'Janine can get her own lunch for once.'

'But——' In the face of his resolution her opposition began slowly, hopelessly to crumble. 'I'd—I'd have to let Janine know. It's only fair——'

'Surely the shop's on the phone? Then ring her.' He took

59

her wrist and pulled her into the hall. 'Dial the number and tell her.'

To her own surprise and fury, Shelley found herself obeying. There was a wail from the other end when Janine heard the news. 'Let me speak to her,' Craig said, taking the receiver.

'Why can't you take me, Craig, instead of Shelley?' Janine's voice came over loud and clear. 'It'd be much more fun.'

'First, young woman, let it be understood that I'm free to choose my female companions. Second, it's not *fun* I'm after. If it were, I'd hardly be taking your iceberg of a sister. Third, the girl never gets a break, so I'm giving her one. So get your own lunch, Jan, and maybe your tea as well. I can't guarantee what time I'll bring Shelley home.'

He turned from the phone. 'What are you standing there for? Or are you waiting for me to collect your personal belongings?'

Shelley was up the stairs and rummaging in her drawer before the question had ended. The swimsuit was yellow and the briefs and top were joined only by a narrow strip of material at the front. It had been an expensive item, bought to wear on her cancelled honeymoon, and therefore virtually new.

She stuffed it into a holdall, with swimming cap and towel, comb and lipstick. 'Come on,' Craig called, 'don't bother to dress up. It's not your boy-friend who's taking you, only me. Not that I object to my women making themselves look attractive for my benefit, but you're not one of them, nor ever likely to be.'

Shelley came to a stop halfway down the stairs. 'If you can't be a bit more pleasant, then call the whole thing off. It wasn't my idea. If it's going to be a kind of penance for you to spend the day with me, and I can see it is, then I'm not coming.'

He was up the few steps that divided them and had her over his shoulder in a fireman's lift before she was aware he had moved. She kicked her legs and as he lowered her to the floor she said furiously, 'Thanks for nothing!'

He grinned and took her bag. 'I like to get my own way.

If I don't, I get dangerous, so take warning.' He showed her into his car. 'Must have been something in my upbringing. You should have a chat with my mother about my boyhood some time.'

'I have better things to do,' she answered, between her teeth.

He laughed loudly, which increased her irritation, and she drew herself as far away from him as she could.

A few minutes later they were heading for the main road and the open moors, which stretched wild and untamed to meet the distant horizon. The day was warm and the sun turned green into gold. It was a rocky, windy ridge they were driving along, with hills abounding, carrying strings of roads and criss-crossed with pathways up and over their summits.

The gradients in places were startlingly steep, even, Craig said, as sheer as one in three, and Shelley held her breath as he manoeuvred the car round hairpin bends with as much ease and familiarity as if he were driving to the shop round the corner. They passed through grey stone villages and crossed bridges over streams and tumbling waterfalls. Sheep grazed by the roadside and everywhere birds swooped and dived and sang.

From high summer into the autumn, Craig told her, heather, masses of it, purpled the hillsides and tamed, for a brief spell, the windswept lonely land.

'Ever been to Runswick Bay?' Craig asked conversationally. Shelley shook her head. 'When the sun's out,' Craig went on, 'as it is today, it catches and holds the warmth. The village is on the southern slopes of the headland. According to a Cleveland historian who lived last century, in 1684 the whole village except one house sank in the night.'

Shelley frowned. 'What happened to the villagers? Were they drowned?'

'No. Luckily some fishermen were operating in the area and helped the inhabitants to escape. They lost their homes, though.'

Shelley was silent, gazing at the scenery as the car sped along. On the horizon was the sea, many miles away, glittering and blue, adding its remote beauty to the sloping, partitioned fields and, above them, the endless, brooding moors.

Craig parked the car and as they stood on the clifftop which overlooked the bay, Shelley caught her breath. Like a great scooped-out basin, the curving, boulder-strewn beach lay below. Creeping down the sharply sloping cliffs were cottages, their white and cream-washed walls brought to vivid life by the brilliance of the sun and the varied colours of the climbing flowers clinging to trellises.

The gardens, small and neatly fenced, were ablaze with carefully nurtured blooms. The pathway down to the beach was steep. Its gradient was such that no sooner had Shelley started to walk than her feet impelled her to run.

Craig caught her up and grasped her hand, steadying her and slowing her down. The sand was soft and yielded to her weight, filling her sandals. Craig pulled her behind him to sit with their backs to a great boulder. 'Relax,' he urged, and tutted when she fussed with her things.

At last she was still and her eyes roamed from one side of the sweeping bay to the other. Craig pointed to the headland extending like a rugged arm into the sea.

'Kettle Ness,' he told her. 'An excellent viewpoint. I'll take you out there some time.' Her heart leapt at the promise, yet knowing deep down it would never be fulfilled. 'It bears the remains of a Roman lighthouse.'

The sea, tamed by the day's calmness, frothed and fingered its lazy way up the beach. A short distance out, a yacht or two, sails white and tall, tacked and rolled. Children, on hands and knees, built sandcastles and scuttled down to the water's edge, returning with slopping pails. People playing beach ball games laughed and shouted.

Craig turned his head and smiled. 'It makes a nice change.' He uttered the platitude with a provocative grin.

'What does?' she parried. 'Coming to the seaside for the day or having me for company?'

'Now would I say it was "nice" to have the company of a girl who detests me?' he mocked.

'No,' she answered flatly.

He rose quickly and pulled her up. 'Join me in the sea. Got your swimsuit in position?'

'No. I'd have to get into it.' She looked round for some shelter.

'Don't worry, I'll leave you to it.' She sank down on to the sand again. He unbuttoned his shirt and flung it down. He unclipped the leather belt around his waist and in a few seconds his trousers joined the shirt on the boulder. His swimming briefs were striped and as Shelley looked up at him, her eyes travelling slowly over the sinewy, muscular legs, almost black with hair, upwards over lean hips and hard, powerful body, desire stirred within her, desire which she thought had died beyond resuscitation the day Michael had gone out of her life.

'Well,' he asked with a derisive smile, 'as a specimen of manhood do I pass?' She coloured and looked away. 'Shy?' he persisted. 'And you once nearly a married woman? Don't try to pretend you're an innocent. That I don't believe.'

She wished he would move. She wished he would drop his jeering attitude, she wished he would take his tantalising body out of reach and let her be. 'Think what you like. Your opinion leaves me cold.'

Her eyes, as she spoke, did not stray from their contemplation of the sea, so when a hand came down and tugged at her drawn-back hair viciously enough to bring tears to her eyes, she cried out.

But in a moment he was gone, wading into the water and submerging out of sight. In her swimsuit, Shelley felt conscious of her vulnerability to the appraising, merciless gaze of the man who had brought her there. A hand to her eyes, she scanned the sea and found that his dark head was a speck out in the bay. The fact that he had removed himself so far from her gnawed at her peace of mind. If anything were to happen to him . . .

What if it did? she asked herself savagely. The figure swimming with such purpose and strength out there meant nothing to her. It was for Janine's sake she was worried, she told herself, creeping with bare, tender-soled feet towards the sea.

Her bathing cap covered her ears and the cries and shouts of the groups around her receded. She waded up to her

63

knees, then plunged and swam, gasping as the chill of the water hit her. Then she settled down to a steady, even stroke, swimming in the opposite direction from the man whose distance from her had only a few minutes ago caused her such concern.

Arm over arm she made for the headland, the high, thrusting ridge of rock and cliff stretching out like a great limb and on which Craig had told her were the remains of a Roman lighthouse. She did not even know the Romans had lighthouses, and thought how clever they must have been to be so advanced in that and so many other ways.

Because her ears were covered, she did not hear the shouts until Craig was almost on top of her. 'Come back, you crazy fool!' he commanded. 'Don't you realise how far out you've come?'

'I'm a good swimmer,' she retorted, turning on to her back and taking deep draughts of air, 'so why the concern?'

'You're a tolerable swimmer. You're not good enough to venture this far.'

'I'll decide that for myself,' she replied blandly, and turned on to her front to swim even farther out.

But Craig was after her and thrust his arm across her back. 'Come back voluntarily or I'll force you back.'

'How,' she gasped, trying to shake him off, 'are you intending to do that?'

'I have life-saving certificates, girl, so I know what I'm doing.' He swam beside her. 'I have my ways, some of them not very pleasant. Now will you do as I say?'

Reluctantly she checked her progress, dived underneath him and came up some distance away. 'Now,' she threw over her shoulder, 'tell me I'm only a tolerable swimmer!'

He came after her but did not touch her, swimming alongside until they were well inshore. Shelley's feet hit the bottom and she stood, gasping for breath, hands on hips.

'You're out of condition,' he taunted, dragging his feet against the pressure of the water. 'You need help.'

In a moment he had scooped her up and held her high in his arms. She shrieked and lifted her free arm, waving it wildly—the other arm she was forced to wind tightly round his neck. He did not put her down but laughed at her plight, so she kicked her legs violently. They overbalanced and fell into the foam and she was pinned beneath him.

The water lapped and licked them, retreating and returning. 'Say you're sorry,' he ordered, pressing her arms backwards into the warm, wet sand, 'say you're sorry or I'll keep you here until you do.'

But his lips came down and prevented her from speaking. The cries of the children, the crunch of foot on shingle, the gentle hiss of lapping waves—all these, Shelley knew, would one day evoke the sweetness and the ecstasy of those moments in Craig's arms on the edge of the sea.

Slowly, taking his time, he eased his exploring lips from hers and she gazed into his mocking, glinting eyes. 'I'm—I'm sorry,' she gasped. A few seconds passed, a lifetime of holding his gaze, unfathomable, mystifying, and she felt the pressure of his body ease. He lifted himself upright, pulling her with him, then he took her hand¯ and they walked across the beach to their boulder.

Craig put out a hand and pulled off Shelley's bathing cap and her hair sprang free. 'Leave it like that,' he said as she moved to pull it in handfuls away from her face. 'For heaven's sake leave the formidable Miss Jenner behind. Give yourself a break. Me, too.' He flung himself on to the sand. 'I like to relax when I'm with a woman, not feel I have to be at my intellectual best all the time.'

She lowered herself beside him and their legs, damp and coated with sand, stretched out side by side. His eyes took a long, hard look at hers, moving appreciatively, uninhibitedly from ankle to glistening thigh. 'Mm, not bad for a man-hating, man-rejected female.'

With a vicious movement she lifted her hand, anger undoing her inhibitions and flinging them to the winds. He moved quickly and she missed. He laughed at her and rested sideways and towards her on his elbow. He lifted an arm, exposing his chest, black with hair.

'Go on, woman, hate me, hit me, get me off your back. Rid yourself of man-hate. And when you've worked it all out of your system, I'll take over.' His voice lowered. 'I'll take *you* over. And when I'd finished with you, you wouldn't know whether you were coming or going.'

65

He laughed at her indignation and she withdrew into herself. Fingers reached out and caught at her jaw, pulling it round. 'You Shelley, me Craig, eh? Pax?'

In the circumstances she could only agree to the truce he had offered and she nodded. His lips brushed hers then they lay silent, eyes closed, side by side, with no part of their bodies touching. They might each have been alone. But although Shelley lay still, her emotions were registering, like a graph on a television monitor, the magnetism that emanated from the motionless body of the man at her side.

'Did you know,' Craig murmured sleepily, 'that this bay is a geologist's haven? All these rocks and boulders strewn about the beach—the geologists come with their little hammers and chip away at them looking for fossils. I'm told they abound on this part of the coast.'

The gulls circled overhead and called their sad call, the waves washed and broke on the shore. The sun streamed down and dried the dampness from their skins.

'Beautiful area, the Cleveland Hills,' Craig went on. 'Did you know it has bred some great men of the sea? The most famous by far being Captain Cook?' He turned his head and then his body. 'Am I boring you?' He reached out and touched her closed eyes. 'Or worse, sending you to sleep?'

She laughed, feeling more relaxed than she could ever remember. 'Do go on, Craig. I've never known a nicer place to be lectured to.'

He sighed. 'She's used my first name at last!' His finger ran down her profile. 'I bet that took some courage.' Shelley laughed again. 'Anyway, lecturing's my job,' he went on, 'and since at this moment our relationship is lecturer to student, you'd better behave. I turn all obstreperous students out of my classes.' He gave her hair another tug, gentle this time, then he lay back. 'A few miles from here there's a village—lovely place—called Great Ayton. Captain James Cook went to school there. The school's a museum now. The cottage he lived in was demolished stone by stone and in the 1930s shipped to Australia. They put an obelisk in its place. That obelisk was hewn from the rock near to Point Hicks. That was the first bit of Australia Cook sighted on his voyage of discovery in the eighteenth century.'

'Tell me more,' she murmured, turned her head and fluttering her eyes open.

He lifted himself on to his elbow again and looked at her. 'Since you've asked me, I will. One of the most useful and sturdiest breeds of horse have come from this region, the Cleveland Bay. Incidentally, "cleveland" means "cliffland" and,' looking round, 'judging by the magnificent surroundings, that's exactly what it is.' He waved his arm vaguely. 'There's ironstone in "them thar hills". The iron and steel industries at Teeside have grown and flourished from those deposits. The waters of the streams run red, not with blood, but with the richness of the local iron ore. Lecture over. My student may relax.'

Shelley smiled but did not open her eyes. A trickle of sand running down the cleft of her brief top brought her head up indignantly. Craig was in the act of scooping another handful of sand and Shelley reached out to stop him, but his arm evaded her, so she sat up and brushed the sand away.

They lunched at the hotel at the cliff top, then ran down the slope again to the beach. Since their boulder had been taken over by a family party, they moved farther round the bay and swam again. This time Shelley dried herself but did not change from her swimsuit. Craig murmured, with a gleam in his eye, 'Now you've finished yourself, dry me.' She looked at him, dumbfounded. 'Come on,' he insisted, 'you must have touched a man before. No woman these days gets to the eve of her marriage without having done so.'

She shook her head indignantly. 'That was different. Michael was my fiancé.'

'And now he's someone else's man. Perhaps if you'd touched him more he would still be yours.'

Under the tan she had acquired she paled. 'Did you have to remind me of my failure as a woman?'

He looked her over. '*Failure*—as a *woman*? You're off your head, my sweet.' He took her hand which held the towel and pulled it towards his chest. Then he lay back.

'Rub me here.' At her hesitation he taunted her again. 'If you don't I shall catch cold.' Shy as a young girl, she rubbed a small area of his skin, but he was not satisfied. 'Now my legs,' he said with a grin. Obediently, and in spite of herself, she moved to his legs, but the feelings the action of drying him aroused made her check herself quickly and throw the towel at him.

He laughed at her flaming cheeks and sat up, rubbing at his wet skin. 'Your sister would have obliged. In fact, she'd have needed no second invitation.'

Her sister! He had to mention Janine. But why not? There was a world, not just a girl, between them. Soon he was still again and Shelley, her eyes closed, thought he must be asleep, but when she opened her eyes to investigate, found that he was looking at her.

She stirred restlessly. What was the meaning of his expression?

'You're desirable, Shelley,' he murmured. 'Are you aware of that?'

Desirable, but not lovable, as she had discovered when Michael had deserted her. 'What if I am? Desire dies without love.'

'Trite but true.'

'As I know from experience.'

'True again.' He watched her face thoughtfully. 'I've seen you as a she-dragon, as a potential bride, as a water nymph,' he gestured towards the receding sea, 'as a highly efficient secretary, as a mother-figure to a small, crying boy. What else are you having beneath that apparently calm surface, those Venus-like curves?'

'Nothing that would interest you.'

'No? *No?*' Hands caught her face, lips burned against hers, but she fought the now familiar—and frightening—rising tide of desire and tried to tear his hands away. They would not move. The lips grew more sure, more possessive, the hands more persuasive and confident. She struggled with all the strength at her command to escape from his tormenting touch, clawing at his hands with her fingers, then, in desperation, with her nails.

He jumped away. 'You vicious little devil!' There was

no mistaking the anger with which he contemplated the scratches, oozing blood, down the back of his hands.

'I'm—I'm very sorry, Craig,' she breathed, 'but—but it was your fault. I told you before,' she lied, 'you leave me cold. No man's going to touch me—or move me to passion ever again.'

'My God,' disgustedly, 'what man would try? He'd need a suit of armour to protect himself when he got near you!'

Timidly, a little frightened, and hating to see the blood she had drawn from his flesh, she proffered her handkerchief.

'Keep it,' he said tersely. 'You might have soaked it in a toxic substance. I'm too young to die.'

His sarcasm, coming after long hours of friendliness, hit her like a slap on the face. He buttoned his shirt, stood up and pulled his trousers over his swimming briefs, zipping the front. Then, without a word, he wandered down to the water's edge. Sadly, because the gold had gone out of the day, Shelley dressed. She was combing her hair when he strolled back. He watched her for a few moments, his expression blank. 'Ready?' he asked tonelessly.

Shelley nodded. They climbed the path back to the car, but not once did Craig, in spite of the steepness of the slope, offer her a hand. The journey home was silent. Janine gave Craig a rapturous welcome. She flung her arms round his neck and he bent his head and kissed her.

Shelley turned away, unable to stand the sight.

'Take *me* out now,' Janine urged.

The bright cheerfulness of the girl who was clinging to him seemed to restore his good humour. 'Where to, for heaven's sake?'

'A walk, a pub, anywhere as long as you take me.'

'Such devotion!' Craig said, uncoupling himself and looking sardonically at Shelley. 'And how different from my companion of the beach.'

'Why, what did Shelley do, Craig?'

'She froze me out, sweetie, and now I'm shivering with cold. If I take you out, will you warm me up?'

The arms were round him again. 'Like this, Craig,' Janine said, pulling him down and pressing her cheek against his, 'like this.'

'A man,' said Craig dryly, looking over her head into Shelley's heavy eyes, 'couldn't ask for more.'

As they left, Shelley said, 'Thanks, Craig, for the outing. I enjoyed it.'

'You could have fooled me.'

Shelley watched them go, her feelings dead. Michael Townley had trampled on her heart. Now, only a few months later, Craig Allard was trampling on her dreams.

CHAPTER FIVE

FOR the remainder of the Easter vacation, Mrs. Allard made a commendable effort to catch up with administrative matters, which meant that Shelley had to make herself available for work every day, and sometimes in the evenings.

She looked upon the few hours she had spent on the beach with Craig—until the moment of their quarrel—as her holiday.

There were a few pages still remaining to be typed of the four chapters Craig had written. After that, he told her, he would not require her services again until he had finished the book.

One evening—the last on which she would be working for him for some time—Shelley was alone in his apartment. She paused in her typing and stared out of the window. Where was Craig? she wondered. Out with Jan, probably. Janine did not always tell her where and with whom she spent her evenings.

The school was empty and silent, as if relaxing in advance of the onslaught which would disrupt its tranquillity the next day but one when the boys returned from their Easter break.

Shelley replaced her spectacles and sighed, flipping through the remaining notes. There were three closely written pages. It was late. She was tired. Should she carry on or postpone finishing the work until the following evening? No, she decided, that would mean another hour spent in Craig Allard's rooms, and that was something to be avoided. She typed on.

All the evenings she had worked for him she had dreaded hearing his footsteps sprinting up the stairs. It was not so much a dread, she decided, trying to rationalise her feelings, as a fear—of his coming near, standing over her and watching her type as he sometimes did if he lingered before going out. But usually those footsteps did not come.

This time they did. Craig was home. But there was another set of footsteps besides his, quicker, lighter, another voice, excited and laughing. It was not Janine's voice, but one which was more mature, more cultivated, more—much more affected. The door burst open and Shelley, startled, stared across the room.

The woman who entered seemed as surprised as she was. 'Oh, so sorry.' Her eyes—large and brown, Shelley noted—sought Craig's. 'Darling, you didn't warn me you had company.'

'Miss Jenner,' came Craig's clipped reply, 'is not company, Sylva. She's typing my book. Haven't you two met? She's my mother's secretary. Sylva, Shelley Jenner. Miss Jenner, Sylva Wallasey-Browne, a friend of mine.'

'Darling,' her palms rested against his chest, 'an old friend, once a close friend.' She turned from him and her hand touched Shelley's outstretched one, then she murmured, patting her hair, 'Darling, where's your bathroom? I simply must repair my make-up.' She felt her lips. 'I do believe you've kissed all my lipstick off!'

Craig directed her and she went in search of a mirror. There was a moment's silence, then Craig wandered across the room and hitched himself on to the desk.

'Well, Miss Shelley Jenner, do you like my taste in women? Your attractive young sister, and the beautiful Sylva? You wouldn't like to add your name to my list?' He drew out his diary. 'How should I describe you? The black-haired, dark-eyed, straitlaced dragon of a woman called Shelley Jenner. Shape, delectable; expression, fearsome; eyes flashing and full of hate. Temper, short; personality, dull; character beyond reproach and likewise dull...'

With amusement he slid his diary back into his pocket. Shelley tore the paper from the typewriter, took up her coat and belongings—and felt his hand grip her arm. 'If you don't like the truth, then tackle the trouble at the source—yourself.' He reached out and pushed her glasses up to the bridge of her nose. 'If you must wear those things, at least let them perch in the right place.'

'Will you leave me alone?' she breathed, conscious of the

72

fact that his guest might return at any moment. 'How can I stay here while you entertain?'

'Have you much more to do?'

'Two pages.'

'Then finish them. It would leave your evenings free again, wouldn't it, to go out with your rather neglected boyfriend.' He regarded her reflectively, tormentingly, exhibiting for her inspection the backs of his hands. 'Every time he touches you do you draw back primly and say,' he mimicked her voice, ' "Don't do that"? And if he ignores the warning, do you tear him to shreds? You see,' he indicated his hands, 'you've left your mark on me.'

Shelley bit her lip, seeing the scars she had caused and feeling with her own body the hurt she had inflicted on him. She started to apologise again, but Sylva returned.

'Darling,' she said, 'I'm dying for a drink.' She looked round. 'If your secretary's in here, where do we go? Your bedroom?' Her smile was deep and inviting, but her host seemed not to notice. Shelley thought bitterly, if I weren't here he wouldn't hesitate. He probably doesn't want an audience, even one who could only listen in on their togetherness.

But it appeared as the evening progressed that Craig did not object in the least to having an audience. He poured a drink for himself as well as his guest, pointedly ignoring Shelley. He shared the settee with his lady friend and when she rested her head against his shoulder, his arm found its way round her waist.

Shelley kept her face averted, but she could not close her ears. They were reminiscing. It seemed by the number of their 'Do you remembers' that they had, during the course of their friendship, thought themselves to be in love. What had occurred to make them change their minds, Shelley could not gather, but it was plain from the trend of the conversation that Sylva Wallasey-Browne was not averse to taking up her friendship with Craig Allard where, not so very long ago, it had ceased.

When Sylva's arms found their way round Craig's neck and Craig's lips were pulled down on to hers, Shelley rebelled. She would not sit there, helplessly, hopelessly,

73

watching a near seduction—of whom, by whom, she did not bother to discover.

She stood noisily, bringing Craig's head round. He disentangled himself from his guest's twining arms and strolled to Shelley's side. 'Finished?' he asked.

'No. I would prefer to complete the last pages in the morning at my own desk before working hours.' Her voice sounded prim, but her feelings were in a turmoil, a fact she had to hide from the man at her side at all costs. So she fixed her face with a stiff, disgusted expression. Let him think her priggish and shocked, she didn't care!

Craig said quietly, 'I should like the notes finished tonight.'

'Then I'll go to my own desk now and finish them there.' Her lips quivered. 'I'm not staying here.'

He shrugged. 'As you wish. But I'd be obliged if you could bring them up to me tonight.'

'Is that necessary?'

His eyebrows rose at her belligerence. 'I'm afraid it is.'

'Darling,' came the seductive voice, 'when you've finished your altercation with your rather rebellious secretary, I'd love a drink.'

Craig did not respond to the request.

'I'm tired, Mr. Allard,' Shelley persisted.

Craig's lips tightened. His hand rested on her shoulder and pressed her down to the seat. 'It would solve all the problems if you finished them here and now. I'll pay you double time if that's what's biting you.'

Shelley's eyes blazed. 'You know it's not. How could you——'

'Dar—ling, I wish you'd stop playing the heavy employer and think about me. Let the girl go. Can't you see she's straining at the leash? Besides,' a persuasive hand reached out towards him, 'with her gone we can be so much more—unrestrained.'

Shelley, provoked beyond words, swept her eyes up to Craig's and engaged in a battle of wills. After that, she would not stay another second...

The eyes into which she was staring narrowed slightly and held hers without a flicker. It was Shelley who was finally forced to admit defeat. She removed the typewriter cover and resumed her typing. Thirty minutes later she was on her way home. But she walked past the lodge and turned into the quiet country lane. She could not face Janine with tears streaming down her face.

To say that she was humiliated would have been an understatement. There was a gnawing pain inside her because of the terrible truth that had hit her with the force of a meteor falling from the sky, leaving a crater where her heart should be. And that truth was that for the whole of that terrible evening, she had suffered the most excruciating pangs of jealousy. That there was only one basic cause of such a destructive emotion she was painfully aware.

It had happened to her again, for the second time in her life. Against her will and entirely against her better judgment she was in love, devastatingly in love, with a man who looked on her with contempt, and who could never take her—or any woman—seriously, even if his life depended on it. And the love she felt this time made her feelings for Michael seem about as warm as a midwinter's day.

After Easter, Muriel Allard went away. Shelley was left in charge again.

With Parents' Day approaching, the extra responsibilities thrust upon her by a headmistress with incurable wanderlust nagged at Shelley's mind like someone driving a car knowing that the brakes were faulty. The pace of work was speeding up and dragging her with it. She began to doubt whether it was within her power to halt the momentum and avoid destruction.

Parents' Day was an annual function, looked upon as important both socially and educationally. Mrs. Allard maintained that it enhanced the school's reputation, thus leading, she asserted hopefully, to an increase in pupil numbers and consequently fees received.

This was the first time, Shelley was informed by members of staff, that Mrs. Allard had vanished from the scene at the run up to Parents' Day. She had, however, promised to return to finalise arrangements. What that promise might mean, Shelley did not even begin to wonder, mainly because she simply had not the time to do so.

Craig kept his distance and this Shelley found to be an even greater strain than her increased responsibilities. He continued to take Janine out, and sometimes Shelley would see him in his car with Sylva beside him.

Occasionally Shelley would take an evening off and go out with Emery. Her attitude towards him had altered a little. She did not hold him at arms' length any more. This he was quick to note and took full advantage of the lowered barriers, stepping over them delicately at first as if they might contain a hidden electrical charge. Shelley was aware of what she was doing. She was attempting to prove to herself that Craig Allard was wrong, that she was not the dull, frigid woman he had accused her of being, that she could attract a man if she chose to do so. Was she also, a whisper said, imagining, as Emery kissed her, that it was Craig's arms she was caught up in and not Emery's at all?

Craig called for Janine one evening as Shelley was leaving the lodge to walk back to the school to put in an hour or two of work. Through the car window he looked at her critically for a few moments and she became conscious, as she always did when Craig was inspecting her, of her appearance. Her glasses were already in place, a hood was tied round her drawn-back hair to keep off the spots of rain which were falling.

Craig called her over to the car, but Shelley objected to his peremptory tone and pretended that she had not heard him. He opened the car door and as she passed, caught her arm, pulling her back.

'I know damned well you heard me, so you can drop the "deaf" act. You look tired. What's wrong?'

In answer Shelley tried to free herself, but he slid out of the car and put himself in front of her, blocking her way. 'Where are you going?'

She answered sullenly, 'To the school.'

'Why?'

'To work, why else?'

Janine came running out. 'Oh, don't worry about her, Craig,' she said. 'Shelley lives and dies for her work. She's

76

there most evenings, that is, when she's not going out with Emery.'

'And how often is she out with Emery?'

'Once or twice a week at the most,' Janine told him.

'Why do you find it necessary,' he asked Shelley, 'to work in the evenings? Can't you get through it during the day?'

'It's Parents' Day that's worrying her,' Janine supplied cheerfully. 'All the arrangements.'

'You're not organising the whole affair yourself?'

'She is,' said Janine. 'I keep telling her she's silly and she ought to write to your mother and tell her she can't manage alone.'

'And have you taken your sister's sensible advice?'

Shelley paused before replying. How could she phrase her answer tactfully? 'I've written three or four times on business matters. I—I haven't had any replies yet.'

He gave a short, exasperated sigh, looked at his watch and came to a decision. He lifted Janine's hand. 'Sorry to have to let you down, sweetie. We'll go out another night. Not now. It seems I have urgent business to attend to.'

'But, Craig . . .' Janine wailed.

Shelley said stiffly, 'Don't let it worry you, Mr. Allard. I'm quite capable of managing the business you regard as urgent. I've managed up to now——'

'And judging by the look of you, had some sleepless nights as a result. Get in the car, Shelley.' He leaned forward and kissed Janine on her pouting lips. 'Always another day, Jan,' he comforted, as if speaking to a child.

'If you think I'm staying in,' Janine said sulkily, 'then you're wrong. I'm going to the tennis club. It's raining, so we can't play, but we'll drink coffee and socialise instead.'

Craig sighed again, long-sufferingly. 'Get in the car with your sister. I'll run you there.'

'There's no need,' Janine said, and flounced away, but Craig pulled her back and bundled her into the back. 'Between them, the Jenner sisters will drive me slowly but surely round the bend.'

'There's no need to play the martyr,' Shelley muttered.

'I don't know why you're bothering,' Janine snapped.

'See what I mean?' Craig asked the rain-spattered wind-screen.

Fifteen minutes later, he was seated at his mother's desk turning page after page of letters, forms and lists. 'It beats me,' he muttered to Shelley, who sat at his side, 'how you thought you could deal with this lot unaided. Bad enough coping with the everyday administrative duties, but to have a happy but entirely unnecessary event like Parents' Day thrown in on top of it . . .' He shook his head. 'Come on, tell me what's been happening to keep you awake at nights.'

Shelley began at once. 'The firm of caterers I contacted said they could fulfil the contract and supply food, staff and so on. The day before yesterday they wrote cancelling the arrangement. Shortage of staff was the reason. Today I managed to contact another firm and they've agreed to do the job. I've had trouble finding florists to arrange the flowers. The firm I wrote to about supplying the three marquees said they had another function to cater for that day.'

Craig groaned and ran his hand through his hair. 'What's this about wines and spirits?'

'We apparently always provide free drinks during Parents' Day.'

'Good grief, I often wondered where the money went that my mother collected in fees. Now I know—back into the parents' pockets, by way of their throats, in the form of food and drink!' He smiled. 'Come a little closer, Miss Jenner, as the cat said to the mouse while they both studied the baited mousetrap, and we'll work this puzzle out together.'

His smile touched an emotional switch inside her and flooded her with warmth. Colour filled her cheeks, brightened her eyes and softened her lips.

'That's better, sweetie,' he said, and her heart leapt at the endearment, even though he had used it earlier that evening to Janine. His hand stretched out and lifted off her glasses. 'Better still. I can't see your thoughts with those in the way.' His eyes lingered then he said, 'Do me a favour, Shelley, loosen your hair. Give me something pleasant to look at while we work side by side deep into the night.'

78

As her hair fell around her cheeks and brushed her shoulders, Craig murmured, 'Thanks,' and dwelt for a moment on her shy smile. Then he turned back to the papers in front of him.

It was nearly midnight when Craig walked Shelley back to the lodge. The place was in darkness. Janine had gone to bed. As Shelley turned to the door and felt for her key, Craig said 'Shelley?' She looked up, her heart pounding.

'Thanks for your help.'

She answered shyly, 'It's I who should be thanking you. I must admit, it was beginning to get on top of me, but I didn't know where to run for advice.'

'Why not me?'

She gazed up at him, but it was too dark to see his expression. They were so close that she had only to lift her hand to touch his cheek. 'You're here to work on your research. I—I didn't like to worry you.'

'Thanks for your consideration, but I am the proprietor's son. And education is my subject.'

Was there a reprimand wrapped inside those words, despite the quiet tone in which they were spoken? Hurt, she turned abruptly, but he pulled her back. 'What's the matter? What have I said?'

'It's not so much what you said as how you said it. Must you always be sarcastic at my expense?'

'No sarcasm was intended, girl. For pity's sake, why do you take umbrage so easily? Is it me, or is it any man? Does friend Emery upset you so easily, or is he, being an artist, more sensitive to your finer feelings than I am? Have you give him the key, but locked out all other males?'

'If you mean am I in love with him, the answer's no. I'll never,' she lied, 'fall in love with any man ever again. How many times have I got to tell you that before you'll believe it?'

There was a long pause, a strangely angry pause. Then he moved the arm with which he was holding her, gathered some of her hair into his hand, twisted it cruelly with his fingers and impelled her towards him. He tipped her face, gave her a hard, swift, careless kiss, released her and walked away.

79

Next morning Craig was at his mother's desk again. Shelley had not expected to see him there and it took a long time for her heart to settle down.

When he called her over to sit beside him, this time to take dictation, its erratic beat started all over again. She realised she would have to take herself in hand, to damp down her emotions. If he continued to do his mother's work, he would often be in the room. She would, she told herself, have to control her feelings better than this.

He gave her a cursory glance, but her glasses were in place and her hair caught back again. There was nothing 'pleasant' for him to look at this morning as he had demanded last night, so his glance did not linger.

'Applications galore,' he grumbled, 'for the post of deputy head teacher.' He thrust the batch of forms aside. 'I'm damned if I'm going to choose my mother's deputy for her.' Shelley handed him another pile of forms. 'Applications,' he read out, 'for the post of teacher of geography,' he took another batch from her, 'of physics,' yet another batch, 'of English. At last a subject I know something about.' He flipped through them but, despite the speed with which he examined them, seemed to assimilate a great deal of information.

'About a dozen that look interesting. The rest you can throw out. While I study these, run away and do some typing.'

It was almost at the end of the morning session that there came a tap at the door. It was so timid and indecisive Shelley and Craig exchanged glances across the room.

Craig indicated with his head that Shelley should open the door. This she did, to find a small sobbing boy standing outside. Shelley looked over her shoulder at Craig and he murmured, 'Trouble?'

She nodded and murmured back, 'It's Jamie Proctor.' She crouched down and asked, 'Jamie, what's wrong, love? Come in.' The child took a few uncertain steps into the room, saw Craig and turned to run.

Shelley caught him. 'Come back, Jamie. Mr. Allard won't hurt you. He doesn't bite!'

Craig, who had strolled round the desk and was looking

down at Shelley, murmured lazily, 'Care to try me some time?'

Shelley looked up sharply. 'Will you be quiet? The last time this happened we quarrelled and you remember the effect it had on the poor little kid.'

'Ah, yes.' He rubbed his chin. 'I remember the cure for the anxiety neurosis you alleged our argument was arousing in him, too. I'm willing to repeat it, if it gives the little boy any satisfaction. It certainly gave this big boy,' indicating himself, 'satisfaction.'

Shelley coloured deeply and muttered, 'Will you behave yourself!'

He grinned. 'But I am, Miss Jenner, I am. You should see me when I'm not!'

Jamie's sobbing had almost stopped, but it started again when he said, 'Teacher sent me.'

'Why, Jamie?' Shelley asked. 'Were you being naughty? But surely you're never naughty, Jamie?'

Craig crouched down, too, grinned at Shelley and said, 'Wrong policy, boy. You'll learn as you get older. Being "naughty" is what makes life worth living!'

'Mr. Allard!'

Craig whispered conspiratorially to Jamie, 'I think she's annoyed with me, don't you?'

A small smile halted the sobs.

'Why have you come, Jamie?' Craig asked.

'The teacher sent me to see the——' he peered past Craig to the desk, 'the lady.'

'You mean Mrs. Allard?' Shelley asked. 'But she's away.'

'The teacher said if she wasn't there then I must see whoever was there. Is that—is that you?'

'No, Jamie, it's Mr. Allard.' She indicated Craig, whereupon Jamie shrank closer to Shelley.

'Come and sit here.' She led him to the secretary's chair opposite the head teacher's. 'Tell us all about it.'

Still clinging to Shelley and talking to her, he said, 'I went to sleep in the lesson.'

'Who's the teacher, Jamie?' Miss White, he told her. Shelley looked at Craig. 'English lesson. She's the English teacher.'

'Is her teaching that bad?' was the amused reply. 'Trust my mother to pick the wrong type!'

'And why did you go to sleep?' Shelley asked the boy. 'Were you tired?' Jamie nodded. 'Why, Jamie?'

'I couldn't help it. I kept yawning—I always keep yawning—and I fell asleep.'

'Aren't you sleeping very well, dear?' He shook his head. 'Why not?' Again he shook his head, indicating that he didn't know why. 'Have you told Matron?' He nodded. 'And what did she say?'

'To stop being a baby and be a big boy like all the others and go to sleep.'

Craig's hand lifted to his forehead.

Shelley straightened and asked Craig quietly, 'What shall I do?'

'Give the woman notice. Fire her.'

'Mr. Allard, please be sensible.'

He sighed and walked round to his own side of the desk. 'Tell me something. How would you deal with it?'

'You really want to know?' He nodded. 'I'd take Jamie out to lunch in the village, drive him to the moors, walk him until he was tired out, give him an enormous tea and bring him back to bed.'

Craig looked at his watch. 'Right. Contact his teacher, explain, get yourself ready and away we go.'

'But, Mr. Allard, I didn't mean it literally. I only meant that theoretically that would be the right treatment.'

'I asked you, you told me. I'm taking you on. Jamie,' the boy looked up at Craig, half fearfully, 'we're going out for the afternoon.'

'You and me?'

'You, me and Shelley here. Want to?' Jamie nodded eagerly.

'But, Mr. Allard,' Shelley argued, 'it would cause a riot. If we do it for him——'

'Don't give me that nonsense!'

'It would be undermining the teachers' authority. How can they impose a meaningful discipline if we reward every child who does wrong?'

'This child was not doing wrong. He was tired, so he, or

82

rather his body, did the only sensible thing. He went to sleep.'

'But, Mr. Allard . . .'

Jamie's blue, anxious eyes lifted to scan their faces.

'Stop arguing, Shelley, and do as I say. At this moment I'm in charge, so you take my orders.'

'Yes, Mr. Allard.' Shelley pressed her lip with her teeth. How he loved slapping her down! She breathed heavily once or twice, calmed herself under his amused gaze, told Jamie she wouldn't be long and left them.

The village boasted a whitewashed, low-beamed restaurant. The meal was substantial and Jamie ate heartily. Shelley did justice to the food placed in front of her, too.

Afterwards they drove in a westerly direction, making for the moors and hills. Craig asked Shelley, 'Ever been up Roseberry Topping?'

She shook her head. 'I like the name.'

'It sounds like cream you pour over your pudding,' said Jamie.

Craig laughed, agreeing with him. 'The name comes from *rhos*, which is a moor or open piece of country, and *berg*, which means a hill. The word "topping" is a local Cleveland word for a hill which comes from the Danish *toppen*, a point or apex.' He pointed. 'Can you see it now? It's just over a thousand feet high.'

From the distance it dominated the landscape, rising high above the other hills and distinguishable clearly by its steeply sloping sides and its overall pointed shape. Craig parked the car and they scrambled upwards to the summit of the hill, Jamie clinging to Craig's hand. Craig offered his other hand to Shelley, who firmly refused it. He shrugged and climbed on.

As they neared the top, the gradient grew sharper. Craig stood, hands in pockets, Jamie at his side, watching Shelley struggle to complete the climb. At last she came to a stop, her lungs clamouring for air, and wondered where she was going to find the strength to join the other two.

She fought her self-respect and lost. 'Craig?' she asked timidly.

But he shook his head. 'Manage on your own. You refused when I offered to help you last time.'

Shelley looked around, judging the terrain. It promised to be a tough and even hazardous final scramble. 'Help me up,' she pleaded, holding out a hand.

'Say, "Please, Craig", then I might.'

She gritted her teeth. 'Please, Craig.'

He laughed, obviously enjoying her humiliation. Nevertheless he joined her and grasped her hand. 'Next time don't be so darned independent.' He pulled her behind him, looking back mockingly. 'I don't like women who say "no".'

'Then,' puffing, 'you'll never like me. I'd never say anything else to you.'

His grip tightened and she winced. 'My dear Shelley, what makes you think I would ever ask *you* a question to which you need answer "no"?'

'No need to rub it in,' she gasped, finding indignation a difficult emotion to sustain while short of breath. 'I'm well aware of my lack of attraction for the opposite sex. I've had it spelt out to me in a way I'll never forget. A woman who's been deserted by her husband-to-be on the eve of her wedding has it indelibly inscribed on her mind.'

As soon as they made the summit, Shelley tugged her hand away. Craig turned his back on her and joined Jamie who was sitting astride a boulder and looking at the view.

It was superb. To the west stretched fields and valleys, green and rich, with farms and their adjacent buildings huddling deep in hollows. To the east, great tracts of climbing moorland, each summit vying with the other to lift higher towards the skyline and reach into the clouds. In the far distance, over the edge of the hills and farmland was the North Sea, its horizon sharp, probably promising rain before long.

Craig said, his arm sweeping widely, 'From the North Sea to the Pennines. From the Vale of York to the hills of Durham. Over there,' his arm moved, 'is Easby Moor. See the obelisk on the top, a thousand feet up? It's a memorial erected to the memory of Captain Cook.'

Shelley found a boulder of her own and sat on it, gazing

around. Jamie, tiring of the view, ran about picking up stones and bringing them to Craig to examine for evidence of fossils. Then, tiring of that, he scrambled down and up slopes just for the fun of doing it.

Craig wandered across to Shelley, looked meaningly at her boulder and said, 'Move along. There's just about room for two.'

Reluctantly, her heart pounding, Shelley obeyed. They sat so close their thighs made contact and Shelley's limbs tingled with his nearness. Hips, arms, shoulders pressed together, and her flesh caught fire where his body touched hers. Casually Craig's arm lifted and came to rest round her shoulders. She found herself pulled closer and more intimately to him. Because of the pleasure that flooded through her veins—no man had ever aroused her to such a throbbing awareness—she stiffened and tried to pull away.

Craig said sharply, 'Relax, woman. I must hold you like this, otherwise you'll fall off.'

'It's not large enough for two,' she complained.

He grinned down at her mockingly. 'All the better. It's my belief that a man can't have a woman too near.'

She jerked with impatience, but he would not let her go. They drank in the silence and the wonder of the view. 'Ever been on the Lyke Wake Walk?' Craig asked. Shelley shook her head. 'You must come with me one day.'

The promise the words held had her heart drumming as if she had climbed the hill twice over. 'One day', months, years, centuries away. She knew that for her the 'one day' he spoke of would never come.

'I'm a member of the Lyke Wake club. The Walk itself stretches from Osmotherley over there,' his arm swung towards the south-west, 'forty miles over the moors and hills to Ravenscar at the coast, over there.' Now arm pointed south-east. 'You walk through wild heather, bracken and bog nearly all the way. To qualify for membership of the club you have to start and finish the walk in twenty-four hours.'

'You mean you walk all night?'

He nodded. 'And all day. You can walk that forty miles without once walking along—only across—any road. It's best to do the walk in June, starting about ten or eleven at night. The worst ups and downs are at the beginning.'

'You didn't do it alone, surely?'

'Good heavens, no. There were a crowd of us. All ages tackle it—a boy of seven and a man of eighty have done it—but not all of them aim to complete the walk in twenty-four fours. Incredible experience. The trees turned red in the rising sun.'

'Did you starve on the way?' She smiled up at him.

His arm tightened and he smiled back. There was something in his eyes that made her feel as if the sun had just risen at the wrong time of day.

'You have a support party who provides you with food, drink and warmth from stoves. At one time it rained, so hard in fact we got soaked to the skin, but we dried out as we walked. The ground was so wet it was like ice. In fact, I fell twenty feet.' He felt her body stiffen with anxiety and he laughed into her eyes. 'So concerned—for a man you dislike so intensely?'

If only you knew, she thought, just what a travesty of the truth that statement was!

'But I scrambled back and continued with the walk. I wasn't the only one who fell that night. We all got through. As you cross the moors you can see the masts and domes of the Early Warning System on Fylingdales Moor. A strange and macabre sight to find in such unspoilt beauty—the four-minute warning of a nuclear attack.'

They were silent for some time and their silence seemed to weld them together more securely than any words they might have spoken.

'I'm hungry,' said Jamie, running up to them and trying to push them apart. The more he prised, the closer Craig pressed Shelley to him. When the pressure of his arms had her gasping for breath, she said, looking up at him,

'Craig, you must stop. What will Jamie think?'

Craig rested his mouth on hers for a few seconds and released her at last, brushing himself down. 'I can't do right, can I?' he asked, good-humouredly. 'When I quarrel with you you say it will upset him. When I cuddle you, you get worried about what he's thinking. Jamie,' he caught the boy's hand, 'never get entangled with a woman. Women, yes,' he grinned at Shelley, 'but "woman", never. In the plural, boy, always in the plural. It's safer that way.'

Jamie, ignorant of the undercurrents and the deeper meaning in the words, nodded vigorously and said, 'Are we going to have some tea now?'

Back in the village they returned to the low-beamed restaurant and Jamie, his appetite sharpened by the hours in the open air, ate an enormous tea.

'Well,' said Craig, as they drove back to the school, 'do you think your cure for this little boy's insomnia has worked?'

'I hope so,' Shelley said. 'When I made the suggestion, I never dreamed you'd take me up on it.'

Craig looked into the driving mirror at the back seat passenger and asked, 'Happy, Jamie?' Jamie nodded energetically. 'Well,' Craig murmured to Shelley, 'you've achieved something—brought a glow to his face instead of tears.'

Jamie climbed the steps back into the school between Shelley and Craig, clinging to their hands. Before he left them, Shelley bent down and hugged him.

'My word,' Craig said softly, 'Jamie's achieved something, too. He's put a match to the iceberg and melted an area, even though it is only the size of an ice cube. Make the most of it, Jamie,' he whispered, 'in a few moments her responses will have solidified!'

Shelley lifted reproachful eyes to the speaker, who shivered and commented, 'I told you so, Jamie. It didn't last. She's frozen hard again!'

Jamie laughed, although he did not really know why, and ran off with a wave. As he disappeared, so did Craig's bantering manner. He consulted his watch. 'Too late now for work.' He looked at her consideringly. 'Would you be willing to come back this evening and tackle the work we left undone this afternoon?'

Shelley felt a stab of guilt. 'I promised Emery——'

'Leave it,' Craig said abruptly, 'forget I asked you. Go out with your boy-friend. I'll work alone.'

'I could put him off.'

87

'Don't even consider it. A girl whose self-esteem has been so damaged by rejection as yours has needs a man in her life for therapeutic reasons, if nothing else.'

'He's not the "man in my life." I haven't got one. We're friends, no more. I don't love him and never will.'

'If I may say so, your outburst sounds a little immature and childish.'

'Go on,' she challenged, stung by his criticism, 'say you don't blame Michael Townley for deserting me at the last minute, that he had a lucky escape.'

He looked her over and there was disparagement in his eyes. 'You might well be right. You're so sour and embittered, I'm beginning to come round to the view that your appeal to the opposite sex has vanished beyond recall.'

CHAPTER SIX

EMERY visited Shelley that evening. They went for a walk, but it began to rain, so they turned back and made for the lodge. Janine chatted to them for a while, but commented with a broad smile on Emery's restlessness.

'I'll be a tactful little sister and find myself something to do. I've brought a wig home from the shop to practise on.'

When they were alone, Emery pulled Shelley close and kissed her. With a feeling of dread, she began to recognise masculine desire and impatience, and knew that she would either have to reject it once and for all, or come to terms with it. She had vowed never to become involved with a man again, except on the basis of friendship. But she was beginning to realise the impossibility of making any man understand that friendship was all she could ever offer.

Craig had said she needed the attentions of a man to restore her self-respect. Perhaps he was right, she thought, allowing Emery to push her back against the cushions, perhaps a man's kisses, uninhibited and passionate, could melt the ice which, ever since Michael's desertion, had encased her emotions. Perhaps Emery, by kissing her like this, could rekindle the warmth inside her and make her attractive again to men, to Craig ...

The living-room door opened. The man in Shelley's mind stood there, watching them. Emery lifted himself upright with a great show of reluctance. Shelley felt her body throbbing with humiliation and embarrassment. How could Craig have walked in like that, as though he owned the place—which, in fact, he did, a small voice reminded her.

'Craig!' Janine was racing down the stairs. 'I saw your car. You told me you were busy tonight.'

'I was,' said Craig, his eyes resting narrowly on the flushed, dishevelled girl on the settee, 'but I found it impossible to work efficiently without secretarial help.'

Shelley stood uncertainly, pushing back her hair which

Emery had loosened. 'I offered to break my date,' she said, trying desperately to regain some of her lost dignity.

Craig replied coolly, 'I never was one to deprive other people of their—pleasures.'

His cold condemnation of her behaviour had her feeling ashamed and indignant at the same time. 'You recommended a man in my life' she wanted to tell him, 'a man to make me less bitter and repelling. Yet when I take your advice, you don't like it.'

'Get your coat, Jan,' Craig said, over his shoulder. 'I'll take you out.'

She was up the stairs in a few moments. Emery picked up his tie, which earlier he had thrown down, and began to put it on.

'No need,' Craig said to him curtly, 'we'll be gone in a few minutes. Then you can continue from where you left off.'

Emery shrugged, sat back and waited. Craig walked to the window and stared out at the massive black rain clouds which were darkening the twilight into premature night.

'I *said* I'd work,' Shelley addressed the broad, rigid back. 'If you'd lifted the receiver and rung me——'

He swung round. 'Let the subject drop. You've every right to refuse to work in the evenings. It's your leisure time and what you do with it is your concern entirely.' He resumed his examination of the outside world.

'But——' Did she have to go on trying to clear herself?

Emery caught her hand and pulled her down beside him. 'Pack it in, Shelley.' His arm, which was round her, shook her gently. 'You're not obliged to work overtime.'

'But we did no work this afternoon, so I really should have——'

Craig turned again and his quelling look bore into her and silenced her more effectively than Emery's hand which had lifted to cover her mouth.

'Let it *go*, Shelley,' Emery said, kissing her lightly. 'I'm the one in luck, aren't I? I've got your company. His loss,' nodding towards the man who was looking at Shelley with near-contempt, 'is my gain.' He whispered loudly in her ear, 'When they've gone, we'll have the house to ourselves.'

Janine raced down the stairs. 'Come on, Craig. Let's leave the loving couple to enjoy each other's company. After all,' she looked impishly into his face, 'you aren't always restrained and gentlemanly when we're together, are you?'

With an odd look of triumph at her sister, Janine swept out, leaving Craig to close the door. As the car drove away, Shelley sat, sickened and empty, resisting Emery's attempts to persuade her to respond to his kisses, and imagining Janine in the arms of the man she, Shelley, loved.

Shelley lay in bed, on the edge of sleep. Janine was home and was probably asleep, too. The doorbell shattered the night's silence, bringing Shelley's eyes open in the darkness and a pounding to her heart. She switched on the bedside lamp, pulled her wrap around her and found her mules.

As she crept down the stairs, the bell rang again, a short, sharp burst. The door was solid wood and she wished with all her heart that she could keep its solidity between her and whoever was on the other side.

There was a shout and the voice was one Shelley heard with relief, a flick of pleasure and just a little fear. 'Shelley! Are you there?'

The bolts slid across, the door creaked open. Craig, dressed as though the thought of going to bed had not occurred to him, said, 'Sorry to disturb you, but we're having trouble with Jamie.' He looked at her ruffled hair, her wrap, her slippered feet. 'Could you get into something warm and come with me? He keeps asking for you.'

'Me?' she asked dazedly. 'But why me?'

He smiled sardonically. 'It beats me why, but you seem to have made quite an impression. The opposite sex are falling around your feet and all you do is scorn them.'

Sarcasm, she thought miserably, even at this time of night.

'May I come in and wait while to get ready?' He stepped into the hall. 'In the circumstances, I'll overlook your lack of welcome.'

She felt the warmth tingle in her cheeks, chasing the fright and fatigue from them. 'I'm sorry, but you gave me a

91

shock. I was drifting into sleep.'

With a cynical smile he glanced up the stairs.

'There's no need to look like that,' she said furiously. 'Emery went home hours ago.'

'Don't shout,' Craig said coolly. 'You'll wake your baby sister.'

Shelley swung round and ran up the stairs, pulling off her wrap. A chunky-knit jacket was buttoned over her nightdress in a matter of seconds, warm clinging pants were pulled on, sandals slipped on to her bare feet. She ran a comb through her tangled hair, started to fasten it back but abandoned the attempt and left it loose about her shoulders.

As she ran down the stairs, Craig glanced at his watch. 'Three minutes—must be a record. I've brought the car for speed. Walking along the drive would take too long.'

A few minutes later they climbed side by side up the steps and into the house. Fatigued and still a little dazed, Shelley stumbled and Craig's arm came out to steady her, leading her into the office.

'Jamie hasn't slept since he was put to bed,' Craig told her. 'Matron swears it was my fault for taking him out this afternoon and getting him too excited. I disagreed and we had a minor quarrel. I said the trouble was there before that. At which point she took offence, saying was I casting doubts on her efficiency and ability to do the job she was paid for?'

'She'll leave,' Shelley warned. 'She doesn't like anyone, even your mother, to question her authority.'

'All right, so she leaves. *I* shall appoint the next matron, and I'll make sure it's a woman with more humanity in her, even if her string of qualifications is only half those of the present matron.' He glanced down at Shelley. 'I called you a she-dragon when I first knew you, but you're like a harmless little pet beside her, for all your abrasive and off-putting ways.'

'Thanks for nothing,' Shelley muttered.

'Keep your cool,' he advised evenly. 'You're going to need it to deal with one Jamie Proctor, small, helpless, lost little boy.' He went to the door. 'Come along, I'll go with you.'

92

Jamie, seeing Shelley creep into the dormitory, held out his arms. Shelley sat on his bed and let him hug her. She smoothed his hair and dried his cheeks. She whispered, 'Tell me what's wrong, Jamie.' But he buried his face in her shoulder.

Craig strolled round to the other side of the bed and watched them.

Shelley held Jamie away. 'Can't you get to sleep, love?' Jamie shook his head. 'Have you told Matron?' He nodded. 'What did she say?'

'She said I was a naughty boy and if I didn't go to sleep like all the others,' he indicated the curled-up sleeping forms of the three boys who shared the dormitory with him, 'she'd smack me and tell my mummy how bad I was.'

This started the tears again and they dampened the ends of Shelley's hair.

'Good God,' Craig breathed, 'I didn't know that. The woman deserves to be fired on the spot! If my mother doesn't come home soon, I'll take matters into my own hands.'

The word 'mother' had Jamie wailing. 'Mummy, I want my mummy!' The words, to Shelley's ears and from this small boy, were painfully familiar.

She looked up at Craig. 'What's his mother doing leaving him here to fret his life away longing for her? It's security he wants, not rigid school discipline.'

'The woman must be hard,' said Craig.

'You're wrong. I've met her and her husband. They're both pleasant and harmless, only wanting the best for their child.'

'For "best" read "status",' Craig commented bitterly.

'It's cruelty to children,' Shelley said, feeling the boy's clinging arms, 'to leave such a sensitive, affectionate little soul in a boarding school environment.'

'It can't be true,' Craig muttered sardonically, 'Shelley Jenner and I agree on something. Don't let the occasion go unrecorded!'

Jamie disengaged himself momentarily and looked at Craig, then at Shelley. In the semi-darkness, Shelley caught the child's worried frown.

93

'Craig, please,' she murmured, looking up at him, 'we mustn't quarrel, not now. It upsets him so.'

Hands in his pockets, Craig considered her pale, pleading upturned face. Then he walked round to her side of the bed, found her chin, turned her face and kissed her, murmuring against her lips, 'Full marks to Jamie. I always did approve of his subtle way of bringing about a pause in our hostilities.'

'Jamie,' Shelley whispered as Craig released her and wishing she could turn down the heat in her burning cheeks, 'you must try to sleep now.'

But Jamie would not loosen his hold. 'Has he had a milk drink?' Shelley asked Craig.

'Yes, I forced that out of the old——' he glanced at Jamie, 'out of Matron.'

'What about something to cuddle?' Shelley hazarded. 'That might help. Have you a teddy bear, Jamie?'

Jamie nodded. 'Matron took it away.'

A suppressed expletive from Craig, then Shelley said, 'My sister's got an old one tucked away. Would you like to borrow that?'

Jamie's face brightened. 'Yes, please.'

'And who,' came the voice from above their heads, 'is going to walk all that way back and get this teddy bear?'

Shelley looked up at him pleadingly. 'You, Craig. Please. It's not far.'

'What?' in a subdued but exasperated whisper. 'You're asking me to walk into your sister's bedroom while she's peacefully and innocently sleeping . . .?'

Shelley caught the sarcasm but merely said, her voice cold, 'It's not in Jan's bedroom. It's in a cardboard box in a corner of the living-room.'

Craig tugged at the neck of his sweater. 'For a moment I really thought you were manipulating events so as to get me into a compromising situation, as a result of which I would have to propose marriage to her. And a proposal of marriage, I vowed years ago, would never, under any circumstances, pass my lips.' He added with a mocking smile, 'Proposals of other kinds, yes, but not—repeat not—marriage.' He walked away and came back. 'Where is this

CHAPTER SEVEN

Two days before Parents' Day, Muriel Allard came home. She entered her office a little shamefacedly, finding her son at her desk.

Shelley stopped typing and her employer greeted her warmly. Then Muriel went to her son's side and kissed him gently on the cheek. Did she hope that such a maternal action would pacify him? If she did, then she had miscalculated, because his frown did not go.

Muriel drew off her gloves and made a little sighing noise, as if to bring to her son's attention the rush and scramble she had just undergone for the sake of her work.

'I got your cable, dear.' The man she addressed did not look up from the letter he was reading. 'I made arrangements at once to return.' He nodded, still without looking at her. 'The plane was late. She threw a quick, uncertain smile across the room at Shelley and pressed on, 'It was so good of you, Craig, to take over my work. I feel so guilty about taking you away from your research.'

Craig said, his voice reproving but gentle, 'Your place is here, Mother. If you open a school and choose to run it almost singlehanded, I think it only right that you should stay at your post.'

'Yes, yes, of course, dear. It's just that I have this urge to move around——'

Craig put down the letter at last and stood up. It was an act, not so much of politeness as an indication to her that he was relinquishing responsibility. 'You'll have to make your choice,' he said. 'Either you give up the school, or you give up your wanderings. When I return to the university in the autumn, you cannot,' he looked across at Shelley's bent head, '*cannot* leave it to your secretary to run the establishment in your absence. The girl nearly went under, which is why I took charge.'

'My dear,' Muriel's voice was full of apology as she

98

teddy?'

'I told you, in the living-room, near the window. You might have to dig down to find it.' She pulled the key from her pocket and held it out. He took the key, caught her hand and lifted it to his mouth, kissing the palm. He grinned, glancing at a staring Jamie. 'Just for the record, to keep a small boy happy.'

'There was no need——' Shelley began, but Craig, who could see Jamie's smiling face, put his finger to her lips.

'There was every need, I assure you. Our truce has already brought about a remarkable change in the object of our attentions.'

'Are you,' Jamie whispered, looking from Shelley to Craig and back, 'a mummy and daddy?'

Embarrassed by the question, Shelley felt Craig's hands settle on her shoulders and as his thumbs rubbed softly against the skin of her neck, her pulses raced and her mouth went dry. Her hands lifted to try to stop him, but he merely imprisoned them under his.

'Why do you ask, Jamie?' she whispered back.

'Because my daddy kisses my mummy like he,' pointing to Craig, 'kisses you.'

Craig murmured, with a goading smile at Shelley, 'We aren't at the moment, Jamie, but one day we might well be. Who knows?'

The answer seemed oddly to satisfy the boy and he sighed and settled back against the pillows.

'I'll get that teddy bear,' said Craig; he bent down and, with his eyes on the boy's tired, small face, kissed Shelley on the mouth. He felt her stiffen, gave her a brilliant, mocking smile and went away.

By the time he returned, Jamie was asleep. The toy was placed beside him under the blankets and Shelley and Craig crept away.

'I'll go home now,' Shelley said as they reached the entrance hall.

'Not before you've had hot drink.'

'I can make one for myself at home.'

Craig shrugged. 'Fair enough. You can make one for me,

95

too. Come on, I'll take you back.'

She pulled away from his arm which was round her. 'You don't have to be so gallant, especially to me. You don't get anything at the end of it, do you?'

'You,' he jerked her in front of him, arms imprisoned like a hostage and forced her towards the car, 'would do well to blunt the edges of your tongue. That is, if you don't want to go to the end of your life unwanted, unloved and undesired.'

'That's exactly what I do want,' she responded fiercely, refusing his command to sit in the passenger seat. She felt herself swept up and deposited there, leaving her dignity on the gravel outside.

A few moments later he had pulled up in front of the lodge and had the door open for her. She got out of the car and said, 'I'm sorry, I can't ask you in. It's too late——'

He gripped her arms and propelled her in front of him again, towards the front door. He still had the key and used it. 'I'm not waiting for an invitation.' To prove it, he entered the hall after her and shut the door behind him, making for the kitchen.

'I said I'd make a hot drink,' she protested.

'If I judge you correctly, you'd make one for yourself and not for me. Since I'm in need of liquid sustenance too, I'll make it. Where's the milk? In the fridge?' She would not tell him but sat instead in a chair beside the kitchen table.

'Thanks,' he said through his teeth, 'for your co-operation.' He asked no more questions but opened doors and drawers, finding cups, cutlery and saucepans. 'I'll entertain you to a meal some time and let you do all the work.'

This moved her conscience, which brought her to her feet, but he waved her away. 'Stay where you are. You might add a poisonous substance to the drink which might make me ill even if it doesn't kill me. You see,' he smiled without mirth, 'I know how much you love me.'

Watching him, she thought miserably, do you?

When the milk was steaming in the cups, he asked, 'Am I permitted to take mine into the living-room?'

'You know very well you are,' she answered, irritation at

his attitude combining with tiredness and making her bad-tempered.

They sat in armchairs opposite each other and the room, showing its years in the chill greyness of the small hours, was shadowed and still around them. Shelley could think of nothing to say. She finished her drink and rested her head against a cushion. How long would he stay? Her resistance was low, worn down by fatigue, his proximity at so intimate a time of night was wreaking havoc with her instincts and breaking down barriers like someone who had gone berserk with an axe in his hands.

Not even with Michael had she felt this longing for arms about her body, lips seeking hers . . . She stirred and opened her eyes to find that his eyes were on hers. There was something in them which puzzled her. Was it pity, compassion? It was certainly not admiration. She shut him out again in case he guessed the effect he was having on her. He had only to stretch out his hand——

'Shelley?'

'Yes?'

'Look at me.' Obediently—she was too tired to rebel—she looked at him. He said softly, 'Know this poem? Second verse? *The mind has a thousand eyes, And the heart but one; Yet the light of a whole life dies When love is done.*'

Tears rushed to her eyes, but he did not move. He whispered, 'Be gentle with yourself, Shelley. Put away your torment. Let the wounds heal and then the scars will fade.' He got up to go, standing in front of her. He repeated, so softly she had to strain to hear, 'Be gentle with yourself, my dear.'

The front door closed behind him. He was not to that the tears which ran down her cheeks were not f man who had run away from marrying her. She had forgotten him. Her tears were for the misery of a empty of the man who had just walked out of the and for whom she represented all that was unlov undesirable in womanhood.

walked across to Shelley, 'I'm so sorry. I had no idea. You should have written to me, cabled me, told me what a naughty woman I was, then I would have come home!'

The two women laughed, but the son of the house did not.

'Mother,' quietly, 'it shouldn't need your secretary to call you home. Your conscience, if not your own interests, should have done that. Here,' he indicated a pile of forms, 'dozens of applications for vacancies on the staff. Here,' another pile, 'applications for the post of deputy head. These *must* be dealt with by you, and only you.'

Muriel sat at her desk. 'Of course, Craig.' She looked up at him, smiling winningly. 'After Parents' Day, I promise to put aside two whole days for studying them.'

'Two days will be inadequate, Mother. With your secretary's admirable help,' Shelley's heart drummed at his praise, 'I've done as much as I could, but there's a great deal more left because I simply didn't have the authority or the knowledge of your own particular requirements.'

'I'm a bad mother, and you're perfectly right to tell me.'

Her son's face softened and Shelley's heart turned over. If he ever looked at me like that, she thought, the barriers I've built so high round my heart would crumble to rubble.

'You're a good mother and you know it,' he chided, 'but as a head teacher of a fee-paying, exclusive school...' He shook his head.

Muriel, whose nature prevented her from feeling too strongly the pricks of conscience or suffering deeply from any sense of guilt, laughed and said, 'Well, you can run away now, dear boy. I've struggled into my harness under your eagle eye, and now I'm rarin' to go. Parents' Day is only two days away,' she pointed out blandly, 'and there's so much work to be done!'

Shelley said, 'Nearly everything has been arranged, Mrs. Allard.'

'It has? My dear, how wonderful! I thought I'd be returning to bustle and hustle, not to mention chaos.'

'With a secretary of the calibre of yours, Mother,' said Craig, 'you should have known that nothing would be left until the last minute, that everything would be tackled weeks in advance and by the time the event was only two days away, everything would be prepared and awaiting only the arrival of the guests.'

'Dear son,' Muriel smiled brightly up at him, 'I'm suitably reprimanded. I always did say that I should hate to get the rough side of your tongue, and now I have, quite rightly. But I've survived, and I love you dearly. Now be off with you! Leave me and my admirable secretary to get on with our work.'

Craig gave an exasperated shake of his head and his mother an indulgent smile. But instead of leaving as she had asked, he went across to the head teacher's 'admirable secretary'. Shelley, out of the corner of her eye, saw him approach and her mouth went dry.

He stood beside her and though he did not touch her, her body leapt in response. She was afraid to meet his eyes in case he read her deepest thoughts, so she kept her head down until he said, 'Shelley?' Her head lifted and wide, apprehensive eyes searched his. Was she going to get the 'rough side of his tongue', too? But it seemed she was not.

'On the evening after Parents' Day, there's a charity dance at the Wallasey-Brownes'. I'm taking Janine and have two spare tickets.' He took them from his pocket. 'Would you like them?'

Shelley drew away as if he were offering her a passport to purgatory. His eyes narrowed. 'Take them, take the boyfriend. They're free.'

She looked up at him, on the defensive. 'Thanks, but I'm not a social creature. Take my sister, don't worry about me.'

'I told you, Craig,' his mother spoke from across the room, 'she lives in that impregnable castle she's built herself into. You won't get her out of it. She's walled up the door.'

'Isn't it about time,' her son said, 'she came out into the harsh light of day? Time doesn't stand still, Miss Jenner. None of us is immortal. Sooner or later age begins to take its toll. Even you, at twenty-five, are not immune to the ravages of time.'

Shocked by the brutality of his words, Shelley lowered

her head to hide her quivering lip. 'I see that every day, Mr. Allard,' she answered huskily, 'every time I look at my young sister, in fact. There's no need for you to remind me of it in such a cruel way.'

'Someone has to scale those walls.' He added, so softly that his mother could not hear, 'Be gentle with yourself, Shelley. Remember?'

She raised moist eyes to his and met a dazzling, persuasive smile that stormed her resolution and blew it to pieces. He held out the tickets again, as if tempting a child into good behaviour with a piece of chocolate. This time she took them.

'You'll come to the dance,' Craig said firmly. 'You're not just putting those tickets aside. That I won't allow.'

'I won't put them aside,' she echoed.

Again that smile, full of persuasion and charm, the smile that touched the very marrow of her bones. His eyes held hers. 'Is that a promise?'

'It's a promise.'

A finger ran lightly down her cheek. 'Mind you keep it.'

'You haven't done the impossible, Craig?' his mother asked as he strolled to the door. 'You haven't persuaded my secretary to join the mad social whirl?'

'Believe it or not, I have.'

'My goodness, she must have had a change of heart since the last time I was home. She was going around as if she had cut men out of her life for good.'

Craig turned at the door. The charm had gone, the customary cynicism had taken over. 'If you'd seen her as I saw her the other night after a tussle on the couch with her boyfriend...'

His mother laughed, but Shelley turned furious eyes on the man who had made the provocative statement. But he deflected her fury with a mocking smile and went from the room.

That evening, before Janine returned from work, Shelley took stock. She examined herself in front of her dressing-table mirror. She was ruthless about it. One by one she took out her illusions about herself and peeled them away, like skin from a fruit, seeing the essence, the flesh, the reality beneath.

And it was that reality which shocked her. It was not surprising that Craig Allard was so critical in his attitude. No wonder, she thought, he took out Jan and Sylva Wallasey-Browne. No wonder that, when he was with her, Shelley, he could do nothing but mock and deride, show pity and brotherly consideration. No wonder, too, that Craig had said, 'Be gentle with yourself.' There was in her eyes a bruised and stricken expression. She looked what she was—a disillusioned, disappointed woman.

Janine came in and ran upstairs, looking for her sister. She asked, 'Did Craig offer you a couple of tickets for the charity dance?' Shelley nodded. 'Did you take them?'

'Yes. Why not?'

'Blast! He won his bet.'

Shelley frowned. 'What bet?'

Janine took off her jacket and swung it from her fingers. 'I bet him you wouldn't accept them. He said you would because you wouldn't be able to resist his persuasive tactics.'

So the tickets had not been offered out of the kindness of his heart. His attack on her withdrawal from social life, followed by a subtle softening of his manner, had all been part of a plot, a strategy to help him win his bet.

'I've a good mind,' she said between her teeth, 'to tear the tickets up. Persuasive tactics!'

'Won't you go?' Janine asked casually.

Shelley answered sourly, 'I suppose you're still hoping to prove him wrong, to win *your* bet? Well, you won't because he got a promise out of me to go to the dance.'

Janine smiled. 'He said he'd do that, too. When he turns on the charm, it's difficult to say "no", isn't it?' She gave her sister an odd, rather self-conscious look and did not answer the anxious question in Shelley's eyes.

'Jan,' Shelley said, changing the subject, 'my hair. Would you be a pet and do something with it?'

Janine stared. 'You're not letting me loose on your hair at last?' She gave a whoop of joy. 'My sister's coming out of

102

her shell! When shall I start? Now?'

Shelley laughed. 'Saturday afternoon, just before the dance.'

'Right,' said Jan good-naturedly. 'Then we'll both look good at the big event. I'll do yours first. You'll have to put yourself in my hands. Promise?' Shelley nodded. 'I won't tell Craig. We'll keep it a secret. It'll give him a pleasant shock. You should hear what he says about your appearance!'

Shelley said weakly, 'What sort of things?'

Janine shrugged. 'That it's a pity you can't run around in a swimsuit all the time, because that's the only thing you look good in. And that someone ought to take you in hand and throw out all your old clothes and buy you some new ones. He even said he'd buy them if you'd let him. Then I said if he's going to buy one of us clothes, it had better be me because I'm his girl-friend, not you.'

'And,' Shelley asked unhappily, 'what did he say to that?'

'Something silly about my not being the only woman in his life.'

Shelley grew cold in spite of the warmth of the June evening. Who, she wondered miserably, were the other women? And was one of them Sylva Wallasey-Browne?

On Parents' Day, the milling, restless mass of people, fond parents, affectionate aunts and uncles and bored brothers and sisters, intermingled and weaved labyrinthine paths, seemingly on collision course, but somehow avoiding disaster.

Shelley looked about her, pausing for a moment to catch her breath. Jamie passed, his hand tugging at the arm of the elegant woman at his side. His face was radiant. A man followed—his father—youngish, benign and with an unmistakable resemblance to Jamie in his features.

Craig came from nowhere to stand at Shelley's side. 'Jamie's mother and father?' he asked. Shelley nodded. 'I'm telling them about the boy.'

She looked at him, aghast. 'You mean about his unhappiness here?'

103

'His bad nights, the crying, the lot. Why shouldn't the parents be told the truth? The child should be taken away from boarding school and sent to a day school nearer home.'

'Let your mother tell them, Craig,' Shelley urged. 'Or Matron.'

'My mother knows nothing about Jamie's troubles. And as for Matron—she'd urge them to keep him here to "make him grow up", as she would so delicately put it.'

Jamie's bright eyes saw Shelley, with Craig beside her. He tugged his mother behind him across the entrance hall. 'There's Shelley,' he shouted, 'and—and Mr.——?' The name had slipped from his memory and shyness threatened to close down on him.

'Craig Allard,' prompted Craig, with a smile. 'Son of the headmistress.'

Mrs. Proctor's hand was offered first to Shelley with a murmured, 'We have met before, haven't we?' and then to Craig, after which Mr. Proctor, a smiling, good-natured man, held out his hand.

'Shelley gave me a teddy bear,' Jamie volunteered brightly. 'I was crying. Teddy told me to go to sleep. So I hugged him and went to sleep.'

Mrs. Proctor glanced uncertainly at her husband. Craig murmured, 'Amuse Jamie, Shelley. I'll deal with this.'

So, holding Jamie's hand and taking him aside, Shelley chatted to him, trying all the time to keep his mind from straying to his parents and the discussion which was taking place between them and the headmistress's son.

Ten minutes passed before Craig joined them, but he was smiling. 'Off you go, Jamie,' he said, and Jamie joyfully obeyed. 'All's well,' Craig murmured, leading Shelley away. 'I explained. Being reasonable, intelligent people they understood. They were grateful to me for telling them. Jamie leaves today. His belongings will be sent on.'

'Your mother won't be pleased at losing him,' Shelley said, turning a little sadly for a last look at Jamie, who was listening earnestly and delightedly while his mother spoke to him. Then he turned a brilliant smile towards Shelley, waved back eagerly and clung to his parents, who were walking away.

'My mother,' Craig said crushingly, 'is a compassionate woman. You should know by now that she puts a child's wellbeing before the money he brings in.'

Shelley's colour was high as she answered, 'I'm aware of that. You're misunderstanding my words. I meant that she would be sorry to see such a nice child go.'

Head in the air, she began to walk away, but his hand on her shoulder detained her.

'How much longer does this affair go on?'

'It's only just begun. There's the presentation of prizes in the hall, followed by speeches which are followed by tea outside in the marquees.'

He said irritably, 'I can stand so much and no more. Speeches and tea be damned, I'm going to my apartment. I'll leave my mother to act the gracious hostess and you,' his eyes flicked over her, 'to your good works. If you want me, you know where to find me.'

'Craig darling!' He was accosted, before he could move a step towards his sanctuary, by a tall, beautiful woman who, with her smile and her seeking, enticing eyes, wrapped her personality around him like a climbing rose round a trellis.

'Sylva!' He looked upon the unexpected guest not with distaste, as he was looking upon all the others, but with relief and, to Shelley's unhappy eyes, uninhibited pleasure.

'Ask me why I'm here,' Sylva said, twining her arm round his. Obediently he asked her. Shelley thought, with disgust, he vows he's immune from women. Women in general, perhaps, and me in particular, but Sylva has Craig Allard exactly where she wants him.

'Because,' Sylva replied, 'my mother has been persuaded by your mother to give away the prizes. You simply must come to the prizegiving, darling. I shall be absolutely bored without you by my side.' Her gaze fixed on his eyes, which he must have found irresistible, because he capitulated at once. 'And afterwards you can take me to tea, Craig. There's no one else here I could bear to spend the rest of the time with. Do come and speak to Mother, darling. She keeps asking me if our affair is on again.' She turned the powerful beam of her eyes on to him.

It's a wonder, Shelley thought sourly, he doesn't cringe

like a prisoner under interrogation.

'See,' Sylva murmured, 'she's looking at us. I'm sure she can hear the wedding bells already!'

Craig laughed and as he walked away, Shelley called, with a sweet, false smile, 'Mr. Allard?' He turned back. 'If I want you, will I know where to find you?'

His brows came together at the spite in her tone. 'I'll be around.' Then he disentangled himself from a protesting Sylva and walked, narrow-eyed, back to Shelley. 'If I were you, Miss Jenner, I shouldn't "want me" too hard. I'm not the marrying kind!'

He watched her smile fade and her eyes cloud over. Then, satisfied, he strode away, to be caught once again in the loving embrace of the girl who, rumour had it, he was once intending to marry.

Emery arranged to call for Shelley to take her to the Wallasey-Brownes' charity dance.

As she gazed at her reflection, Shelley was forced to acknowledge that she looked her best. Gone was the drawn-back unflattering hair-style. Janine had used her scissors to the greatest advantage, shaping it and setting it so that it tapered to rest attractively at the nape of the neck.

The long dress had been costly, but the effect it had on her looks had made it worth every single pound she had paid for it. The white crêpe of which the dress was made was scattered here and there with great sunbursts of black flowers making a dramatic contrast to the white background. The back plunged open to the waist, the front as low as it dared. But it was the cut of the dress which lifted it into the near-couture class. And it was the cut which showed to the world the shape beneath the surface and which, according to Janine, Craig Allard had admired when, and only when, it had been clothed in a swimsuit.

Craig came for Janine before Emery arrived. Shelley stayed in her room, but even the sound of his voice touched off her pulse rate, like the shriek of an alarm clock. Her whole body was stirring as if from a long sleep. Desire—for the praise of one man, for his compliments and admiration; to feel that man's passion arousing hers so much more skilfully, more profoundly than Michael's had ever done—was awakening in her a longing which was crying out—quite hopelessly, she told herself—for satisfaction.

But Craig had warned her—'I'm not the marrying kind.' She hoped fervently that he had given Janine a similar warning.

Janine ran up the stairs and burst in at the door. She looked good, too, in her long floral dress which, in Shelley's eyes, revealed her youth and vulnerability far more than the casual clothes she usually wore. Shelley hoped that when the time came, as with a man like Craig it must come, he would let her down lightly.

'We're going, Shelley. Emery's late. I suppose he hasn't forgotten?'

Footsteps climbed the stairs and Shelley panicked. 'See you there,' she said to Janine, and pushed her from the room. Craig mustn't see her now. He would only mock her and demolish at a glance all the self-confidence she had so laboriously built up.

She turned the key and leant against the door as if to keep out a dangerous intruder. 'What's the matter?' came the taunting question. 'Afraid of me?'

'I'm not on show,' she called.

'And why should I want to look at you while I've got Janine to feast my eyes on?'

Even through a solid, ancient door he was deriding her and managing to batter down her self-assurance.

'Oh, go away,' she called, 'go *away*!'

'My dear girl,' he called back derisively, 'I'm going. I wouldn't touch you even if I were hanging over a ravine and you were the only person in sight to cling to!'

It was not until the front door slammed and the car drove away that Shelley was able to overcome her anger and right the self-respect which Craig Allard, with a few neatly chosen words, had knocked sideways.

But when Emery saw her he gave a loud and expressive whistle. 'You might have told me,' he said, 'I'd have brought my sketch book and pencil and committed all this dazzling beauty to paper.'

'There's no need for you to make fun of me,' said

107

Shelley.

'Make *fun* of you? Girlie, in that dress you're devastating.' He kissed her. 'What do you say, we stay home and make love?'

She laughed at the sheer audacity of the suggestion.

The door of Shurwood Hall was opened by one of the Wallasey-Brownes' domestic staff. Shelley's coat was taken from her and a ticket given in exchange. With Emery beside her, she stood in the doorway of the great room which had been added to the house by the present owners. The room had been designed to blend tastefully with the grandeur of the nineteenth-century mansion. The lighting was modern, however, and the paintings around the walls the works of modern artists.

The master of ceremonies, dressed in scarlet and black, bent his head and listened for their names. Then, in a powerful, commanding voice, he informed the chattering, laughing guests that Miss Shelley Jenner and Mr. Emery Slade had arrived. Emery moved on and Shelley's eyes were drawn by a waving hand to the excited face of her sister. Beside her was Craig, his eyes riveted on the girl who now stood alone in the doorway.

Shelley's gaze held his, but the blackness of the sky at night would have told her more than the eyes that were now staring into hers from the other side of the room.

Emery, realising that his partner was not beside him, turned back to find her. He stretched out a hand and Shelley put hers into it. 'Your sister's getting agitated,' said Emery. 'We'd better join her.'

'Shelley,' said Janine, 'that dress—wow! Craig, isn't she great? I did her hair. We kept it as a surprise. And the dress, it cost a fortune!' She shook her partner's arm. 'Say something, Craig.'

'I'm deprived of speech,' Craig responded with a flicker of a smile, and his sarcasm, in place of the praise Shelley had been longing to hear, was like grit thrown into her eyes.

'You can save your breath,' Shelley told him levelly. 'I know exactly what you think of me.'

'Is that so? You can read my thoughts?'

Janine laughed. 'I told her what you said about her. It did her good. She went out and bought that dress and let me cut and style her hair.'

Craig's eyes went on their travels over the face and figure of Janine's sister, coming to rest for a long moment on her hair and then her eyes as if conducting a safari into the jungles of her mind.

'Drink, Shelley?' was all he said.

'Let me,' offered Emery. 'You provided the tickets, I'll buy the drinks.'

Craig shrugged. 'Fair enough. Go with him, Jan. He'll need help.'

Janine made a face but trotted obediently after Emery. Craig turned to Shelley and looked her over reflectively. 'You know, if I were really hanging over that ravine, dressed as you are, I might—just might—let you rescue me. With such a beautiful woman willing and eager to rescue a man from death, what man would want to die?'

Now she had his praise, it grated on her ears. 'What makes you think,' she hissed, 'that I would *want* to come to your aid?'

He laughed. 'Maybe you're right. Even if I were to stop breathing, I can't imagine you giving me the kiss of life!'

Emery and Janine returned with the drinks and Janine chattered to Craig and to Emery, having given her silent sister up as hopeless. The music began and Craig put down his empty glass.

'Come on, young Jan,' he said. 'Translate all that energy you're putting into talking into dancing instead.'

Emery said, 'Let me take the most beautiful girl in the room in my arms.'

Shelley gave Craig a quick, triumphant glance. 'Your compliment's a bit extravagant, Emery,' she gave him a dazzling smile, 'but I love you for it.'

'You do?' His arm grasped her waist and pulled her close. 'I'm making headway at last. I'll think up a few more as the evening goes on, and by the end of it you'll love me so much I might even succeed in making a dent in your armour!'

'No need to wonder,' said Craig dryly, 'where that might

get you.'

Shelley coloured and said defiantly, 'No harm in wondering. And don't bother to curb your imagination!' She watched Craig's eyes narrow, but held his gaze boldly.

'You see,' Emery joked, 'she's even giving me some encouragement. Sweetheart,' his lips touched her ear, 'dance with me and we'll talk it over.'

Craig drew Janine amongst the dancers and Shelley followed Emery. Emery asked, 'What's going on between your sister and the headmistress's son?'

'They're friends,' Shelley answered shortly.

'You're kidding! The word "friend" no doubt being a polite expression for——' Shelley tripped. 'Hey,' Emery exclaimed, 'my poor feet!'

'Sorry, Emery, I'm out of practice.'

'Out of step, you mean.' His cheek found her hair. Craig and Janine passed and Shelley caught Craig's taunting smile. She jerked her head free and Emery protested but did not repeat the action.

Janine was gazing up into Craig's face as though she adored him. Now and then he smiled down at her, but there was no admiration his glance, just an indulgent fondness. Shelley felt she could tear him apart. He had Janine eating out of his hand. One day, Shelley knew, that hand would be snatched away and Janine's heart would be splintered beyond repair as her own had been.

The music ended and Emery said, 'I'm ready for another drink. Come with me,' he tugged her hand, 'and I'll treat us both.'

So they made for the bar and stood there drinking. An acquaintance of Emery's drifted over and introductions were made. They talked and laughed, but Shelley took no part in the chatter. Her eyes wandered and hovered over the moving, interchanging groups. There was Mrs. Allard looking gay and lively in a long pale blue dress. Shelley lifted her hand to return her employer's greeting.

A slim, gracious woman whom Shelley recognised as Mrs. Wallasey-Browne passed from one laughing, animated circle of people to another, attaching and detaching herself, elegant, practised hostess to her fingertips. She was fol-

110

lowed closely and doggedly a footstep or two behind by a benevolently smiling, grey-haired man with a military bearing. He was, Shelley assumed, Mr. Wallasey-Browne.

There was a pause in the music and the dancers rested. Surrounded by men and leaning languidly against the wall was Sylva Wallasey-Browne. One of her group was Craig Allard. His elbow was propped against the wall and a hand supported his head. His legs were draped one over the other and his free hand rested negligently on his hip. He was gazing down at Sylva as if the sight of her beauty, so near, so tantalising, was all he could ever ask of life.

He must have felt the tug of Shelley's regard, because his eyes flicked up and, as they encountered the sullenness of her expression, narrowed estimatingly. For all of ten seconds their gaze held, then Craig straightened himself, murmured a few words to the girl beside him and strolled, hands in pockets, across the room.

Shelley, seeing him approach, looked wildly round for somewhere to run, but the dancing had begun again and no obvious sanctuary could be found. Her glass was taken from her and a hand caught hers. Without a word Craig led her to the dance floor and swung her into his arms.

If her heart would stop pounding, if her body, pressed to his, would become compliant instead of moving with the stiffness of a penguin, if the touch of him did not make her responses leap and burn like a forest fire, she might, she told herself, be able to rise to his high standard of dancing.

'So,' he said softly, 'the beautiful princess has left the fastness of her castle and come out at last into the light of day.'

She glanced up at him, remembering the smile on his face as he had looked at Sylva and compared it with his mocking expression now. She asked, her voice brittle, 'How many drinks did it help you utter that compliment?'

The mockery was wiped clean away and the eyes holding hers iced over. 'No wonder your bridegroom turned and ran! He probably got so fed up with trying to find any responsive womanliness in you he went into the arms of another in sheer self-defence.'

'I knew,' she muttered furiously, 'you were ruthless and

callous and a womaniser, but I didn't know until now that you were spiteful as well!'

He disengaged himself from her and walked away, leaving her alone and forsaken in the midst of the dancers. He made straight for Sylva who, a few moments later, was secure in the arms which only seconds earlier had been round Shelley.

Shelley pushed her way through the crowd to the door, her lip painful between her teeth, her eyes brilliant with tears. The cloakroom was empty and a sanctuary, a place where she could fight for control and somehow regain it.

She wanted to stay in hiding until the dance was over, to run out of the house and walk in the evening sun across the moors, to go home and lock herself and her misery in her room.

Emery would be wondering where she was, so she left the peace of the cloakroom and returned to the dancing. In the entrance hall there were a few couples, talking, kissing, huddled into corners. There was no sign of Emery. His friends had dispersed. Sylva was still in possession of Craig. Their dancing was almost professional, their steps perfectly matched. They chatted, laughed, showed every sign of a return to the intimacy they were alleged to have shared a few years before.

It was then that Shelley saw Emery. Janine was dancing with him, and gazing into his face with something that seemed to Shelley to be near desperation. Now and then Janine would glance at Craig and his partner, then return to talk even more animatedly to Emery. If she was hoping to make Craig jealous, then she was failing lamentably. He was totally absorbed in the girl with whom he was dancing.

'Shelley, my dear,' Muriel Allard called. Shelley turned and Muriel patted the empty seat beside her. 'You're all alone. Come and talk to us. Nan,' to Mrs. Wallasey-Browne, 'meet my wonderful secretary, Shelley Jenner.' Mrs. Wallasey-Browne inclined her head. 'She's an angel,' Muriel went on, 'she positively runs the establishment when I'm not there—which,' she admitted unabashed, 'I must confess is pretty often, isn't it, my dear?'

Shelley nodded faintly.

'Have you eaten, Miss Jenner?' Angus Wallasey-Browne enquired. He occupied the seat on the other side of Shelley.

'I—I'm not particularly hungry,' Shelley told him.

'Nonsense. I'll get you some food.' Moments later a plate overflowing with savouries and sandwiches was thrust into her hand, while into the other was pushed a glass. 'Eat, drink and be merry, Miss Jenner,' he said, laughing heartily at his own joke. 'They'll fortify you for the remainder of the night's dancing.'

Shelley looked about her. Considering that the man who was alleged to be her partner seemed perfectly happy in the clutches of her sister, and the man in whose arms she longed to be was oblivious to the rest of man—and woman —kind in the embrace of his ex-girl-friend, there was small chance of her dancing again that evening, unless some un-attached, bored male invited her to do so.

Shelley ate the food Mr. Wallasey-Browne had so thoughtfully provided. When the rhythm of the music changed to an old-fashioned waltz, Mrs. Allard said,

'Angus, do invite my charming secretary to dance. I can't think what's wrong with all the young men tonight. Look what they're missing!'

Angus Wallasey-Browne needed no second invitation. As Shelley circled the floor with him—many of the younger people had opted out—she was conscious of Craig's mock-ing smile as she passed him by. Sylva, who was clinging to his arm, waved to her father and joked with him about 'cradle-snatching'.

The group of dances finished and a more modern rhythm took over. Shelley returned to her seat and Angus mopped his brow. 'It's a long time,' he commented, 'since I've part-nered a sprightly young wench. It takes it out of me!'

Craig was pulled towards the floor by Sylva, but Janine smoothly cut in and claimed him. From the discussion which followed, it seemed to Shelley that he had been asked to choose. His hand fingered Janine's chin and after con-sideration, he kissed Janine on the lips but took Sylva on to the dance floor.

Janine flounced away and grabbed Emery again. Emery went gladly and Shelley reflected that he seemed to have forgotten her existence. Three dances later, Craig was lounging against the wall again, a drink in his hand, when his mother called him over.

'Craig dear, whatever are you thinking of? Here's my delightful secretary sitting with us old ones, when she ought to be romping with people of her own age. Dance with her, Craig. She looks so lost sitting here.'

Craig considered her, taking his time, his eyes hard. Shelley's face was flushed with embarrassment, her eyes bright with hope. Her hands gripped each other moistly and her whole body waited for his invitation.

He swallowed his drink and asked her if she would like her glass refilled. She shook her head and smiled shyly, expectantly. He walked away.

His mother tutted. 'Well, I don't know. He's a bad young man and when we get home I'll tell him so. Where's the partner you came with, dear?'

Shelley indicated Emery who was still dancing with Janine. She could not speak for the tears which were gathering behind her eyes. Craig had taken Sylva's hand and now they were together again.

Mrs. Wallasey-Browne watched them speculatively. 'It looks, Muriel,' she commented thoughtfully, 'as though we might be linked by your son's and my daughter's marriage after all. How long do you give it before they announce their engagement?'

'Tonight, I'd say,' Angus put in jovially. 'By heaven, they're going it, aren't they? Hope they don't dally too long, Muriel. We've got to know the wedding date well in advance. We'll have to start making arrangements on the spot.'

'I wonder where they'll honeymoon?' Nan Wallasey-Browne mused.

Shelley rose, smiling wanly at her companions. 'Please excuse me. I have a dreadful headache.'

'Cool off in the cloakroom,' Mrs. Allard advised.

'Ask the housekeeper for a tablet, Miss Jenner,' Nan offered. 'She'll know the kind to give you.'

'Misery, isn't it,' Angus sympathised, 'having to be sociable when you're not feeling up to scratch?'

Shelley thanked them for their kindness and made her

114

way to the door. In the cloakroom was solitude and a place to hide her burning cheeks. She had not recovered from Craig's humiliating rejection. It would be hard, if not impossible, to forgive him for the pain he had inflicted, for the insult of his deliberately turned back and his slow, lazy steps walking away.

The woman in charge of the cloakroom took her ticket and handed Shelley her coat. 'Leaving early, dear?'

'Headache,' was all Shelley said.

The door was opened for her by another guest and she walked along the drive, leaving the music, the dancing and the party spirit behind. Outside in the cool, sweet-smelling night air was tranquillity, if not peace of mind.

She was almost at the end of the drive when a car drew up.

'Where do you think you're going?' Craig's voice cracked through the driver's window.

'Home,' she snapped.

'Thumbing a lift?' he enquired sarcastically.

'I'm walking.'

'Get in the car. I'll take you.'

'I'd prefer to walk.' She lifted her head high and walked a few steps, but Craig flung open his door and was after her in a few seconds, catching her by the shoulders and jerking her round to face him.

'Come off that pedestal, lower your well-shaped nose and do as I say.'

'I told you,' she struggled, 'I prefer to walk and *I'm going to walk!*'

'Are you coming quietly,' he asked, holding her easily despite her twisting wrists, 'or do I have to manhandle you?'

'You are already,' she said tearfully, and ruefully rubbed at her flesh where his fingers had bruised.

She went quietly then and allowed him to see her into the car. 'Tell me,' he said, driving on to the main road, 'why did you allow your boy-friend to be hijacked from under your very nose by your sister? Don't you care about the man enough to be cat-like back and use your claws to hang on to him?'

'Janine wasn't acting like a cat. Anyway, I was sorry for

115

her. You deserted her. She had to have someone to take your place. I watched her and could see how upset she was. She was hiding her heartbreak——'

His loud laugh cut her off. 'Heartbreak? You're joking. Let's put it bluntly. She was making a play for your man, and he wasn't being exactly unco-operative, either.'

'How can you talk about Janine like that? You're treating her as I was treated. You're no better,' she stormed, 'than the man I nearly married. A woman has only got to look at you in a certain way——'

'Isn't it time,' he broke in, '*you* looked at a man in a certain way? Isn't it time you lost your dignity, your "I'm too good for you" attitude?'

'If you knew the agony I went through,' she answered, self-pity swamping her, but he broke in again.

'It never occurred to you, I suppose, that the trouble might have been within yourself?'

She covered her ears. 'Stop probing and reminding me of things I want to forget. I'm not in the market for a man any more, so what does it matter if Janine does take Emery away? All this analysis and dissection, as if my emotions were something that can be cut up on a laboratory bench! And,' she turned on him, 'how can you set yourself up as judge and jury of my behaviour with men when yours with women doesn't stand up to examination?'

He made no reply.

'You're not the marrying kind, you told me, yet you've been playing around with my sister for months.'

'Jealous?' he taunted, turning right into the drive leading to Mapleleaf House and pulling up outside the lodge. 'Would you rather I played around with you? Just give me the signal, the age-old signal that a woman gives a man she desires...'

Shelley wrenched open the car door and slammed it behind her. She raked with frantic fingers for the key, hoping to get into the house before Craig could stop her. But he was too quick for her fumbling fingers. He swung her round and had her pinned against the door, his arms on each side of her. In the moonlight his face was taunting.

'Why don't you leave me alone?' she cried. 'I don't want

116

any man mauling me about, especially you. Keep your womanising activities for women like Sylva. Don't degrade me with your attentions!'

His lips disappeared, his eyes glittered. 'My word, you're a sour, acid-tongued shrew, and I'm not taking that sort of abuse from any female, let alone you.'

He seized her by the arms, his fingers digging into her flesh. He pressed his body down so hard she had to fight for breath. His mouth crushed hers, forcing back her head painfully against the wood of the door. His lips were savage and merciless, reducing her to limp, yielding submission. Her hands sought and found his waist. She had to hold on to him, otherwise she would have sunk to the ground.

At last he lifted his head, but he did not let her go. She started crying, she couldn't stop herself, her whole system was so shocked. She sobbed, 'B-be gentle with m-myself, you told me.' She lifted brimming eyes. 'Isn't it time you were g-gentle with me?'

He gazed at her in the moonlit darkness, he looked a long time. Then he murmured, 'So it's gentleness you want, is it? I've got plenty of that, too.'

When he gathered her into his arms, she went without resistance. She had none left. If he had lifted her and carried her into the house she could not have stopped him. His lips were soft and seeking and drew such a response from her that she knew, even in her relationship with her ex-fiancé, that she had never reached the heights to which this man, if he ever chose to do so, could take her.

Reason stirred, began to assert itself and finally took command. This man was 'not the marrying kind'. Nor would she ever let herself consent to be one of his women, only to be thrown aside when another took his fancy. She had, by desertion, been turned into one man's cast-off. It must never be allowed to happen to her again.

She indicated by the increasing rigidity of her body and a drawing away of her lips that she wanted him to stop. Slowly he straightened and his hands fell away.

'I'm sorry,' she said in a tight voice. 'The answer's no.'

With a hard, narrow glance at her face, he turned and went away.

CHAPTER EIGHT

A WEEK after the night of the dance, Muriel Allard announced that she was off on her travels again.

'Don't tell my son till I've gone, dear,' she told Shelley. 'I know he'll oppose my going, but he's so immersed in his writing and researching he won't even notice my absence for a day or two. He's kept to his room lately and I've only met him now and then at breakfast.'

Shelley had not seen Craig, either. Since the dance he had stayed away from her, but was it only his work, Shelley wondered, that had made him keep his distance?

Shelley asked, hiding a frown, 'Where are you going this time, Mrs. Allard?'

'I shall fly to Paris and then make up my mind. Don't worry, I'll let you have my address in case anything urgent crops up. But you can cope, can't you, dear? You always have done before. And,' brightly, 'you can always ask my son to help if a particularly difficult problem crops up.'

Shelley's heart sank. Work with Craig again? No, she would rather struggle against any odds than call on him for assistance, even if it meant working the clock round seven days of the week.

'Now,' said Mrs. Allard, 'this camping trip with the boys at the start of the summer holiday. Mr. Lightfoot, the physical education teacher, usually takes them. They're the boys, you know, whose parents are abroad and unable to send for them for a week or two after the end of term. To keep them occupied, we arrange for them to camp for a few days.' She picked up a piece of paper. 'Unfortunately, Mr. Lightfoot has sent me a note informing me that this year, for the first time, he's unable to oblige.' She put down the letter and looked consideringly at Shelley. 'Have you ever been camping, dear?'

If Shelley's heart could have sunk any lower, it would have done. Now what was Mrs. Allard going to ask of her?

'No, I haven't,' Shelley answered. 'Why, Mrs. Allard?'

'The thought just occurred to me ...'

Shelley knew she was now supposed to ask, 'What thought, Mrs. Allard?' so she did.

'That you might enjoy taking those dear little boys this year. It would be such a change for you, plenty of open air and exercise. You've been looking a little pale lately, you know. I think you need a change.'

A rest, Shelley thought, not a change, a rest from unhappiness and the strain of loving a man who doesn't return my love.

'I don't think I could manage on my own,' she began, but Mrs. Allard cut in,

'I would never have dreamed of your going on your own. I was thinking of——' She paused. 'Haven't you a young man amongst the staff? That nice art teacher, Mr. Slade? He would go with you, dear, I'm sure he would! In fact,' she picked up the internal telephone, 'I'll ask him now.'

Before Shelley could stop her and say, I haven't agreed to go myself yet, Muriel was in touch with the staff-room and asking to speak to Emery. The conversation lasted a few minutes and when it was over, Muriel was smiling.

'He said he would be delighted to accompany you. The time is well in advance of his own holiday, which is just fine.' She sighed with satisfaction, as if she had pulled off a big financial deal.

So next day Muriel Allard went away, leaving her desk piled with unfinished work. Shelley, with immense reluctance, took her place once again at the headmistress's desk. At least, she thought wearily, the new members of staff had been appointed, except for the deputy head. This last appointment Muriel had decided to postpone until the start of the autumn term.

Shelley carried the weight of the administration on her sagging shoulders, longing to run to Craig for advice and assistance, but denying herself the luxury even of phoning him. Janine had not seen him lately, either. His book seemed to be occupying him to the exclusion of everything else.

Emery visited Shelley one morning. He hitched himself

119

on to the headmistress's desk and said, 'What's all this nonsense about taking some perishing little boys camping?'

Shelley looked up with surprise. 'If you feel like that about it, why did you agree to go?'

'What else could I say to the old girl? She put me on the spot. You were taking them, she said, and would be all on your own, and since I was friendly with you, I was the obvious choice. What could I say to that? Politely decline the invitation and let my girl-friend go hang? I could just visualise you struggling singlehanded with that little lot. I know how Lightfoot's come back exhausted every time he's gone.'

Shelley's heart began to submerge again. 'I'd rather you didn't come, Emery, if you're going to come reluctantly. It just wouldn't work that way.'

What am I saying, she thought, talking him out of it so that I'd have to cope on my own? But he said, 'Don't worry, I'll go with you. For old times' sake, if nothing else.'

What, Shelley wondered, did that mean?

'Come on,' said Emery, 'place those cold lips against mine and thank me nicely.'

Shelley smiled and reached up, pulling his head down to give him a light, quick kiss—and the door opened. They broke apart and stared into the narrow, flinty eyes of the headmistress's son.

Emery slid off the desk and rambled self-consciously past the newcomer. 'See you later, Shelley,' he said, and the door clicked shut.

Craig, who was wearing no jacket and had partly unbuttoned his shirt in the heat of the afternoon, came slowly across the room to stand beside Shelley, towering over her. She looked up nervously, feeling like a juvenile delinquent who had been caught committing a crime while out on parole. That he was going to make the most of her agitated state there was no doubt.

'Good thing I came in when I did, isn't it?' he asked curtly. 'If I'd delayed my entrance by no more than a few minutes, I'd have found you flat out on the desk entwined in your boy-friend's arms.'

Slowly the colour rose in her cheeks. His proximity, his arrogant good looks, the magnetism that emanated from him making her want to reach up and pull him down as she had pulled Emery, temporarily deprived her of the power of speech. After a few moments she managed a halting, 'I'm sorry.'

He had, it seemed, decided that he had reduced her to a sufficiently abject state because he changed the subject, asking abruptly, 'Where's my mother?'

Which presented yet another problem—how to tell him where his mother was without exacerbating his already simmering anger.

She temporised with, 'She's not here, Mr. Allard.'

'You have a genius for stating the obvious, Miss Jenner. I'd be grateful if you would enlarge on that statement.'

Shelley could not remain seated. It made her feel at too much of a disadvantage, so she urged back the chair and stood, unsteadily because in putting her head that much nearer to his, she had also placed it within snapping distance—and that he would now proceed to do his best to snap it off she had no doubt.

It was necessary to avoid his eyes, because to look at him in his present mood would be to reveal to this merciless man just how much she was afraid of him.

She said hoarsely, 'Your mother's abroad, Mr. Allard.'

There was a long pause, then, 'So she's gone again, leaving you in the hot seat?' Shelley nodded. 'Why wasn't I informed of her departure?' Shelley was silent. 'You're her secretary. I'm sure she must have told you to tell me.' Shelley held her breath. 'Which means you "forgot",' he smeared the word with disbelief, 'either deliberately, to annoy me, or accidentally, which reflects on your proficiency as a secretary.'

Shelley looked down at the pile of letters she had been attempting to answer. Her refusal to respond must have infuriated him, because his hands came out and he swung her round. 'Will you answer me!'

She kept her emotions under iron control, emptied her face of all expression and told him, 'She's gone to Paris. She said she would inform me of the address at which I

121

could communicate with her whenever necessary.'

The hands gripping her shoulders were beginning to hurt. 'You still haven't answered my question.'

Shelley's head lowered as she murmured, 'Your mother told me not to tell you until she had gone.'

The hands moved away. 'I see. When did she go?'

'Last Monday.'

'Four days. Why didn't you tell me earlier?'

'You were busy with your writing.'

'You could have interrupted me to tell me that.'

If she told him, I didn't want to bring you down here to do your mother's work because then I would have had to work with you, and the last thing in the world I want is to have you near me . . .

'I decided to try to manage on my own.'

'And can you?'

She raised her head. 'Yes, thank you.'

He walked to the window and gazed out at the flower-filled gardens. 'I'm at a crucial stage in my book.' He turned. 'Could you carry on a few more days?'

'I can carry on indefinitely, Mr. Allard.'

He gave her a look which told her that he did not believe her. 'By that time,' he continued, 'I should be free to take over down here. Until then, if you could carry the bulk of the work and come to me for advice and, if necessary, help whenever you need it, I should be grateful.'

'I won't trouble you, Mr. Allard.'

He came close. 'You're damned sure of yourself, aren't you, Miss Jenner?'

There was no possible answer to such a question, so Shelley did not attempt to find one. He looked at her for a moment and went out. Shelley sank on to the chair and held her head. She had discovered one thing—there was no such sentiment as forgiveness in the whole length and breadth of Craig Allard's body.

Janine passed her hairdressing exams. She was so delighted she decided to have a celebration party.

'Who's doing the catering?' Shelley asked dryly. 'An outside firm?'

Janine put her arms round Shelley's neck. 'My sister Shelley's a good cook. She'll bake some cakes if I ask her nicely.'

'But, Jan,' Shelley removed the arms that were threatening to choke her, 'I'm so busy at school at the moment, with Mrs. Allard away.'

'All right, I'll make them myself.'

Shelley sighed. 'You know you're atrocious at cookery. You're pushing me into a corner, aren't you?'

Janine grinned. 'Yes. I knew you were a good, kind sister . . .'

'How many are coming?' Shelley asked resignedly.

'Ten, perhaps more. A few from the tennis club, a couple of the other hairdressing assistants and their boy-friends.'

'Don't go on,' Shelley groaned, 'or I'll withdraw my offer of help.' She paused. 'What about Craig?'

'Oh, I expect he'll come,' Janine said airily. 'You'll be asking Emery, won't you?'

'Why? It's your party.'

Janine smiled. 'To keep you company, of course.'

'You make me feel like an old granny! You think I'm going to spend my time sitting in the corner knitting and looking on indulgently, while you "kiddies" play?'

'Yes,' said Janine, and Shelley threatened her with a plate she was washing.

Janine said casually, taking the plate from her and drying it, 'Mrs. Caversham said that now I've passed my exams, I can have that partnership in the business, provided I can put some money into it.'

Shelley frowned. 'How much money?' Janine told her. 'We haven't got that much to spare, Jan. I'm sorry, I only wish we had.'

'But you've been working overtime a lot lately, haven't you?'

Shelley smiled at her sister's bland assumption that any money she, Shelley, earned, was Jan's to dispose of at will.

'I have been working overtime, Jan, I agree, but I certainly haven't been paid for it.'

Janine dried the plate over and over again. 'But surely we've got some savings tucked away?'

123

'For "we" read "you",' said Shelley, 'meaning me, of course. Yes, I've got some savings, not a great deal, but I put them aside for emergencies and holidays, not to mention new curtains and so on. I don't see how I can give that money to you, Jan, much as I'd like to.'

'There must be a way,' Janine said, her face like that of a small girl who has seen a beautiful but unobtainable doll in a toyshop window.

'I'll have to think about it,' Shelley told her. 'In the meantime, you'd better make a list of guests for your party. If it's too long, you'll have to trim it, won't you?'

Shelley kept her promise and baked the cakes for Janine's party. Janine made the savouries and sandwiches. Both Emery and Craig were coming, Emery's acceptance being definite, Craig's provisional. Pressure of work, he said, might keep him away.

The party was in full swing and still Craig had not arrived. The guests had been asked by Janine to provide their own drinks and in this they had obliged liberally. Music was provided by a record player brought by the boy-friend of one of Janine's colleagues.

Shelley danced for a while with Emery, but did not enjoy it. There were too many people in the small room to make dancing enjoyable, although the others seemed to thrive on the closeness. Shelley slipped out into the kitchen unnoticed, even by Emery. He was too busy dancing, gyrating and swaying opposite Janine to notice Shelley's absence.

The coffee had to be made, cups and saucers assembled and trays filled with food. Janine was either supremely ignorant of the work going on behind the scenes, or deliberately forgetful of all the preparations a party involved. Shelley thought it was the latter, and felt she could not blame her. It was her party, after all, in celebration of her achievement.

The knock at the door had Shelley's heart knocking, too. There was only one other guest to come. Craig gave a brief, ironic smile as he saw Shelley's apron, her fingers stained with red from the beetroot she had been slicing, and the flushed, hard-pressed look about her.

'Cinderella?' he asked. 'Sitting amongst the cinders while little sister plays?'

'Someone has to do the work,' Shelley muttered, returning to the kitchen. She added over her shoulder, 'The party's in the living-room. Please go in.'

But Craig strolled along the hall and propped himself against the kitchen doorway. 'If the party's in the living-room, what are you doing here?'

She snapped, buttering scones, 'I'm not in a party mood.'

'Still mourning your lost love?'

Shelley did not answer.

'Why isn't anyone helping you?'

'I suppose by "anyone" you mean Jan. It's her party. She's enjoying herself.'

'If she's all that happy in here,' nodding towards the living-room, 'without my company, what am I doing here?'

'You mean why did she invite you? As her boy-friend, perhaps?' Shelley smiled at the tomato sandwich she was making.

'Hell, no. Wrong age group.'

She looked at him with some surprise. 'You say that after going around with her for months?'

He lifted the shoulder that was not resting against the door frame. 'A pleasant way of passing the time. She's good to look at and stimulating company.' With a provocative smile, 'Unlike her sister. Cheerful disposition—again, unlike her sister.' He saw her lips tighten. 'Why the irritation? You consider I'm denigrating you?'

'I'm used to that from you. Anyway, why should I worry about what you think of me?'

He thought a moment, then, 'Ah, I know why you're needled. Because you object to the way I speak so casually of my relationship with your sister. You'll be starting in a minute on your favourite topic, that I'm breaking her heart and condemning her to a life of man-hate like her jilted sister.'

Her eyes flashed up to his, which were laughing. 'Will you please go and join the party?'

He did not move. 'If I'm so important in her life, then why did I see her getting on so well with your boy-friend as

125

I passed the window just now on my way to the front door?'

'What do you mean, "getting on so well"?'

'She was sitting on his knee and had her arm round his neck.'

'They—they've probably had a bit too much to drink.'

'Well,' he folded his arms, 'it's as good an explanation as any—in the absence of the truth.' Shelley looked up at him questioningly and saw his jeering smile. 'Can't keep any man, can you?'

She threw down the knife and flung herself on him, but he moved swiftly and had her wrists imprisoned in a punishing grip. 'My word,' his eyes narrowed expectantly, 'there's fire in that body as well as a brain in that head. I seriously started wondering how far I could go before you began to show how much you hate my guts. So the man who walked out on you hasn't completely dewomanised you after all, and stripped you entirely of self-respect.'

'Let me go,' she said, her breath catching in her lungs.

'What, let you loose to tear me to bits with those claws? Look at them, curled and grasping all ready to draw blood.'

The living-room door opened and he let her go. Her wrists were red and sore and she rubbed them, flexing them to restore the feeling and movement. 'You hurt me,' she muttered tearfully.

He folded his arms again. 'And you asked for it. The next time you throw yourself at me, I won't just hold you off. I'll give you *more* than you're asking for.'

'Craig, you came!' Janine came flying out from the midst of the party and flung her arms round his neck. 'Come and dance with me!'

He held her waist. 'Shouldn't you be out here helping your sister?'

'She'd only tell me was in the way. Come *on*!' She pulled Craig behind her and he seemed to go willingly enough.

Shelley finished the sandwiches and arranged them on a plate. She could hear the throb of the music and over it, the laughter and shouts of the dancers. Cigarette smoke drifted into the hall and as she loaded the trolley with food, she heard a shriek.

Janine rushed out of the room. 'A cloth and lots of water,' she demanded. 'There's Coke on the carpet.' Then she rushed back into the room.

Shelley groaned. She found the necessary cleaning materials and took them amongst the crowd. While Shelley got down on her hands and knees, everyone stood in a circle and watched.

Craig's voice above her head asked, 'Who spilt the Coke?'

'Confess, confess,' one of the young men shouted.

'I did,' said Janine.

'Then don't you think you should be down there cleaning up instead of Shelley?'

'It doesn't matter, Craig,' Shelley murmured, but she felt herself lifted by two strong, determined hands and put aside. The cloth was taken from her and pushed into Janine's hand.

'Get on with it, sweetie,' said Craig, his voice light but edged with a quiet authority. 'You did the dirty deed, you clear up the mess.'

Some of the men clapped ironically. 'That's right, keep the women in their place,' one of them said, and ducked as the girls threatened to set upon him.

'But, Craig——' Shelley remonstrated.

He put his hand round the back of her neck and marched her from the room. But instead of leading her into the kitchen, he walked her to the foot of the stairs.

'Get up there, woman, take off that schoolmarmish blouse and skirt I swear I've seen you wearing at work and wriggle yourself into something attractive. The more tight-fitting it is, the better the men will like it, and I'm no exception. I've seen you sunbathing on the sands in next to nothing, so I know just what you're hiding underneath all this camouflage.' He tugged at the neck of her blouse, but Shelley wrenched herself free. She tried to turn and dive beneath his arm, but he moved and blocked her escape.

'If you don't go of your own accord,' he threatened, 'I'll carry you up and keep you under surveillance until you've done what I say, whether I offend your maidenly virtue or not!'

With great reluctance, she climbed the stairs, turning once to see if Craig had gone, but he remained in the hall watching her. There were some purple velvet pants hanging in her cupboard which Janine had bought for her months ago. They had stayed unworn because she had felt she could never rise to their demands. They followed her outline too faithfully for her peace of mind. Now they clung like a second skin. Janine had bought a white round-necked top, slashed across with wide horizontal purple stripes to match the trousers. This also fitted her well—too well, Shelley thought, as she studied her profile in the long mirror.

Strange, she thought, as she combed her hair and applied some make-up, I feel a different person. Not as I used to feel when Michael loved—she corrected herself—when I thought Michael loved me. But more—feminine was the wrong word. Female, she told herself, I feel more female ...

As she crept down the stairs, hoping to slip into the kitchen unnoticed, she saw Craig at the same moment as he saw her. There was a long, thundering silence. The thunder was the blood pounding through Shelley's veins as she saw Craig's expression.

After a long, long time, he murmured, 'My *word*! I feel like Professor Higgins in *Pygmalion*. I've produced a woman, and my God, what a woman!' He said softly, 'Come down here, Miss Jenner.'

Slowly, almost terrified of what he would do—if he so much as touched her she would scream—she complied. Now they were face to face as she paused on the bottom stair. His hands were in his pockets. As she stepped down into the hall, she knew an overwhelming feeling of desire. She wanted those hands to slip out of hiding and grip her as they had gripped her in the kitchen when she had tried to batter him, to slip round her and hold her, never letting her go ...

But those hands stayed where they were. Only his eyes bridged the gap between them, soaking up her image like blotting paper until it spread and covered the entire area. He did not touch her. He could make as many comments as he liked, but the fact remained that she was still not attractive enough to make him want to reach out——

'Shelley! Darling!' Janine hugged her. 'You're wearing the things I gave you. At last you've had the courage to put them on. What do you think of her, Craig? Isn't my sister great? I haven't seen her look like this since Michael——' A hand to her mouth. 'Sorry, Shelley. I meant for ages.' Over her shoulder, 'Emery, come and see your girl-friend now. Grab her quick before someone else gets the idea!'

Emery came and Emery grabbed, with both his hands. He pulled Shelley into the living-room, turning one of the men out of an armchair and occupying it himself, pulling Shelley on to his knee.

Janine turned to Craig. 'I want to sit on your knee.' She tried to tug him towards a chair which a girl had vacated, but Craig would not move. 'What's the matter?' Janine asked plaintively. 'I've been on your knee before. Why not now?'

But Craig had his eyes on her sister, who was now caught tightly in the clutches of the man on whose lap she was sprawled. 'Come on, Shelley,' Emery was saying. 'You've held me off long enough. I'm a frustrated artist champing at the bit. In that come-and-get-me outfit, you can't still pretend you're made of stone.' He placed a kiss on her lips and held them.

'Craig!' cried Janine, excited by the sight of her sister in Emery's arms. 'Kiss me like that.' She added childishly, 'After all, it is my party.'

The others laughed, but Craig said, his eyes hard, 'If you want me to make love to you, sweetie, we'll do it in private.' Shelley struggled free of Emery's mouth and tried to sit upright, but Emery held her down. She turned her head to look at Craig, hoping somehow to convey to him that she had been forced into the situation against her will.

But Craig eyed her cynically. 'Heaven knows, I'm not inhibited, far from it, which is exactly why I'd rather do it without an audience. Then I can really let myself go.'

'Come on, then, Craig,' Janine said happily. 'Upstairs——'

'Jan!' Shelley said sharply.

Craig remarked, eyes narrow and spiteful, 'Your big sister's warning you off me, Janine. In her eyes, I'm an immoral, dissolute lecher who uses women for his own ends and then throws them aside.'

'Man, what's wrong with that?' asked one of the men from his horizontal position on the floor. Everyone laughed again, everyone but Shelley. She struggled once more to get away from Emery and this time succeeded, standing up and straightening her clothes.

'I'll get the food,' she said, and came up against Craig, who was blocking the doorway.

She felt the hardness of his body against hers and her desires—those desires which had been battered into senselessness by the brutal suddenness of Michael's desertion—were rekindled into clamouring life. Their eyes met and the tension in his limbs were reflected in his look. Somewhere deep inside him there lurked a strange kind of anger, but anger which was held rigorously in check.

What had she done to annoy him? Any moment, she thought, edging past him, his hand would come out and grip her as Emery's had done, but more viciously and without Emery's playfulness. But she was allowed to go by and he made no attempt to touch her.

He did follow her, however, but was silent as she made the coffee. She wished he would speak. She knew he was watching her and her cheeks grew warm, her actions jerky and self-conscious, her heartbeats heavy and hard. If his eyes could have this effect, what would the touch of his hands do to her?

But she fought her emotions and the response he could arouse simply by being in the same room. She fought for rationality and detachment, because there was something she had to ask him.

'Craig?' she said uncertainly, her eyes on the work she was doing. He was so silent she looked up at him. His expression hardly encouraged her to go on, but she braved his dark, brooding eyes and asked,

'Have you—have you any more notes ready for me to type? I mean the book you're writing?'

'Sorry, no.' Her disappointment was too obvious to be

ignored and he asked sharply, 'Why?' She said it didn't matter, but he insisted on an answer. She said with a shrug, 'I just wanted to earn a bit of extra money.'

For a long time there was no reaction and Shelley, who had not dared to look up, wondered what was going through his mind.

'Am I permitted to know why?' he asked at length. Now she was silent, but he persisted. 'For yourself? For a holiday, perhaps? Or clothes?'

'For Jan,' Shelley replied. 'Now she's qualified, Mrs. Caversham's offered her a partnership in her hairdressing business, provided Jan can contribute some money as a partner.'

He walked across the kitchen and confronted her. 'Let's get this clear. You're actually intending to earn money in order to give it to your sister, to subsidise her career?'

She looked away uncomfortably. 'That was the general idea.' Then, challenging him, 'Is that a crime? That I should want to help my sister? Who else is there, if I don't?'

'She couldn't earn the money for herself, of course?'

'She could, but at her rate of pay it would take her years to accumulate the amount Mrs. Caversham seems to want.'

'She could spend less on clothes, couldn't she? Each time I see her she's wearing something different, unlike you who dresses in the same sackcloth and ashes day after day.'

'How I dress is irrelevant,' she said sharply, ignoring the pain his words had inflicted. She could hardly say to him, Your mother pays me so poorly I haven't enough money left over to buy myself clothes.

'It might be to you, but it isn't to those who have to look at you all day.'

'All right, so don't look at me!'

'My dear girl,' he drawled, 'I look at you as little as possible. Except when you're dressed like that. You should wear those clothes more often. In that outfit a man can really see what you're made of.' His eyes raked her from top to toe.

'So,' she said, turning away to hide the high colour his scrutiny had induced, 'you haven't any work I could do?'

131

'I've told you already,' he said quietly, 'no. What do you want me to say—yes, there is some—work you could do for me?'

Their eyes met and as she saw the meaning in his her whole body burned with embarrassment and anger.

'Even if you offered me work now,' she snapped, 'I wouldn't take it, not even if you said you'd pay me treble what you were paying me before!'

She pushed the trolley past him along the hall and into the living-room.

Craig walked into the headmistress's office next morning. He was holding a letter and it was plain he was in a bad mood. Now what have I done? Shelley wondered.

But for once it was not the headmistress's secretary who had provoked his ill-humour. It was the headmistress herself.

Craig threw the letter on to Shelley's desk. 'From my mother. Read it.'

Shelley picked it up and obeyed. 'Craig dear,' Mrs. Allard had written, 'I've met the most charming man. He's an ex-major, like your father was. He hasn't an abundance of money, but he's certainly not poor. His manners are impeccable, his background public school, Oxbridge and the army. Who could ask for more? I'm thinking of marrying him, dear. I'm sure you'll have no objections, because he's so right for me you could find simply nothing to object to. Do write and tell me you approve of my plans. I shall feel so much happier if you do. A letter will find me at the address above. My hotel room and the Major's face each other across the passage.'

Shelley handed back the letter. Doubts and anxieties began to stir at the back of her mind. Change was threatening, the future was no longer as certain as it had seemed only a few minutes before.

Craig sat in his mother's chair. He smiled sardonically. 'You'll notice the way she puts it.' He quoted, ' "I'm thinking of marrying him." It probably hasn't occurred to the poor devil yet that such a fate could await him. Shall I write to the man warning him?' He pushed the letter back into the envelope. 'After all, I have a fellow feeling for him. If I do nothing, another man will go to his doom. You see,' his smile was deeply cynical, 'I don't believe in the married state. I'm on my guard all the time. If I weren't, how could I have reached thirty-five without burdening myself with a wife?'

Shelley flushed and turned back to her work. He said, picking up a pencil and scribbling on his mother's blotter, 'But you obviously believe in marriage. You were on the brink of it yourself once.'

Shelley frowned down at her work. 'I learn by experience. I don't believe in it any more.'

'What about your current boy-friend?'

'Emery Slade? There's nothing between us.'

'No? How can you speak for him? I saw the look on his face as he pulled you into his arms last night.'

'Mere physical desire,' she tossed at him with a careless shrug.

He laughed loudly, ironically. 'Such cynicism from such an unsophisticated, unsullied young woman! Or,' narrowly, 'aren't you as innocent as you seem? I must be honest, I've often wondered.'

'I'm astonished you've wasted any time even thinking about me. Anyway,' with a move as if to end the conversation, 'I'm a cynic these days. Past events have hardened me.'

He gave a short unconvinced laugh and went out.

A few evenings later Craig called for Janine. Shelley was flicking her hair into place in front of the living-room mirror when he came in. He greeted Shelley with a slow, lazy smile and she hastily pushed the comb into a drawer.

'Don't mind me,' he drawled. 'Carry on beautifying yourself. Who's it for, anyway? Surely not in my honour?'

Why did he always manage to put her at a disadvantage? 'For you?' she asked with exaggerated incredulity. 'As if I'd bother! Anyway, even when I'm in the same room as you, you don't even see me——' She checked herself too late.

He came nearer. 'You'd like me to "see you"?' He

caught her arms and pulled her close. 'To touch you, even? Just give me the sign, lady, and I'll oblige, willingly and with the utmost speed. I may not believe in marriage, but by heaven, I believe in all that goes with it. If it were offered to me free, with no conditions, no strings, I'd be the last to shake my head.'

She chided herself for having given him so much encouragement with such an unguarded remark. She twisted away from him, rubbing her arms where his fingers had gripped her. 'If I were giving any "signs" as you call them,' she said furiously, 'you would be the last person I'd choose to signal to!'

'What's the matter with you two?' Janine asked, coming into the room and breaking into the hard silence like someone smashing through a pane of glass. She glanced at Shelley, 'I can see you've put her in a bad mood, Craig. And Emery's coming. What did you say to her?'

'*I* say to *her*?' with mock innocence. 'She's being rude to *me*. I called her a she-dragon once. I wasn't far wrong. Every time I talk to the girl she breathes fire and gnashes her teeth.'

'Then the answer's simple, Craig,' Janine said cheerfully. 'Just don't talk to her. Come on, you're taking me out, aren't you? Or are you going to spend the whole evening fighting with my sister?'

'Just give me the chance,' Craig murmured with narrow, glinting eyes, 'just give me the chance!' He turned and followed Janine into the hall.

Shelley was almost ready for bed when Janine returned from her evening with Craig. Her eyes were glowing, her whole body radiated happiness.

Shelley's heart plunged. Surely, she thought, pulling on her wrap, Craig hasn't proposed? But the proposal Craig had made was of a very different kind from the one Shelley had been thinking of.

'Craig's giving me the money Mrs. Caversham wants for a partnership in the shop,' she said, flinging down her coat and hugging her sister. 'I won't have to wait years or even months. Look,' she ran across to her bag and pulled out a

134

cheque, 'there's the money, all of it. He said pay it into my bank account and then write a cheque for Mrs. Caversham.'

'You mean,' said Shelley slowly, sinking on to the bed, 'he's lending it to you?'

'Lending it? No, *giving* it. It's a gift, he said. He said it was no use lending it because he knew I'd never be able to pay it back.'

Shelley lifted a hand to her forehead. 'He—he can't do that. Unless,' her voice wavered, 'unless you're——' She found it impossible to finish the sentence.

But her sister had no such scruples. 'Unless I'm sleeping with him?' She laughed loudly, then she shrugged. 'I wouldn't tell you if I was, would I? I'm over age, Shelley, so stop trying to act the heavy parent. Anyway, you can say what you like,' she pushed the cheque back into her hand-bag, 'I'm keeping this.' She turned at the door. 'One day I might pay it back, but I'm certainly not going out of my way to do it.'

Next morning, Shelley pushed her way through a moving mass of boys going to assembly and climbed the stairs to the top floor of the house. She rapped on Craig's living-room door, but there was no reply. Another series of raps brought a growling response, not from the door which she was almost denting in her assault on it, but from another room.

The voice called, 'Wrong door. Try the one on the left.'

The handle turned and Shelley found herself in a bedroom. The curtains were drawn against the sunlight. Clothes had been flung in a heap on a chair. Dressing-table, chest of drawers, in fact every available surface, was covered with books, papers and folders.

In the bed along one wall, Craig lounged, hands behind his head, blanketed up to his waist. The rest of him was uncovered. Shelley saw the latent strength in the upraised arms, the breadth of his shoulders and the ridge of his collarbone standing out rigid and hard below his neck.

She was transfixed, not so much by the sight of him as her own reactions. The strength of them appalled her, because they revealed to her the extent of his attraction for her. 'Animal attraction,' she told herself desperately, 'nothing more. I mustn't love the man like this. I must hate him instead for what he can do to me.'

He smiled at her, a slow, lethargic smile. 'I had a late night,' he explained. 'Not with a woman but with a book. After I left your sister I felt the urge to work.' He saw her frown. 'What's the matter? You're not trying to tell me you've never seen a man in bed before? And you almost a married woman? Come nearer, I won't eat you.' She moved slowly towards him and stopped a step or two away. His eyes skimmed over her. 'Not in that prim and proper secretarial uniform you're wearing. And those spectacles sitting reprovingly on your nose.' He watched her agitation with amusement. 'Well, you've invaded the seclusion of my bedroom. There must be a reason.'

'You know very well what the reason is. The money you've offered my sister——'

'Not offered, sweetie, given.' The endearment, spoken so lazily, so carelessly, made her heart jerk.

'Thank you for *offering* it, but I'm sorry, she's unable to accept.'

His expression hardened. 'She's already accepted.'

Their eyes did battle, but Shelley could not bring herself to fight to the finish. She looked away, took a breath and said, 'All right, we can regard it as a loan.' Now she looked down at him. 'Every penny of it will be paid back.'

His eyebrows shot up. ' "We"? I was under the impression the money was given to your sister, not you.' He rolled on to his side and propped himself on his elbow. 'Let's get this clear. Your sister is over age. She can make her own decisions with or without your approval. I've given her the money, she's said, "Yes, thank you." There the matter ends.'

'No, it does *not*! If she doesn't pay the money back, I will. I insist——'

His free hand shot out and caught her wrist. 'Relax, girl. I refuse to argue in bed.' He jerked her nearer. 'There are so many other, better things one can do in it!'

Shelley tried to pull her wrist from his fingers. 'What's the matter?' he asked, and watched as her eyes moved down his body outlined so clearly beneath the covers. 'I'm decent below the waist, if that's what's worrying you. I'm wearing pyjama trousers. Since my mother's away, I'm a kind of father figure to the precious inmates of this flaming school she's burdened herself with, so I can't dress—or undress—quite as I please.'

'All the same, I *will* pay the money back——'

He twisted round on to his back and tugged her down so that she was lying on top of him. She struggled frantically but without hope of escape, and he laughed at her efforts. 'Come on, girl,' he whispered, 'let yourself go.' He removed her glasses and put them on his bedside table. 'You're a woman, you're warm, responsive...'

'No, I'm not,' she cried, her voice muffled by the soft hair on the rock-hard chest against which her cheek was resting—there was nowhere else to put it. 'I'm just an intelligent automaton. You hate clever females, you told me so.'

She stayed still because she had no alternative. She had no more breath with which to carry on her struggles. His arm was an iron band across her.

'Intelligent automaton,' he mused, lifting her chin so that he was looking into her eyes. 'No, it's a contradiction in terms. An automaton functions automatically without thinking, whereas intelligence requires thought. The two just don't go together.'

In spite of herself, Shelley relaxed, delighting in the rough feel of him against the smoothness of her skin, the power of the muscles that held her captive. He relaxed, too, his hold around her slackening and becoming caressing. For a few ecstatic moments she yielded to his touch, her whole body turning traitor. Her hands lifted and rested against him, feeling the softness of the flesh on his shoulders, the hardness of the bones beneath. With a shock it came to her that she had only to turn her face up to his, let him see the capitulation and longing in her eyes...

Catching him off guard, she twisted and writhed, finding the floor with her feet and slipping like an eel from his grasp. As she broke free he made a grab at her, but she eluded him, snatching her glasses from the bedside table, ramming them on and racing for the door. Momentarily she turned back. His smile was broad and mocking.

'You'd better make sure no one's around to watch you leaving my bedroom. You know what they'll think, don't you? And if you'd stayed on top of me only a few moments longer, they would have been right! Your hair's in a mess, your blouse has slipped from its moorings,' hastily Shelley tucked it into the waistband of her skirt, hiding her bare midriff, 'and if that wasn't enough to give the game away,' he turned on to his side and gazed at her calculatingly, 'your eyes are brighter than I've ever seen them and your whole face is alive.' With a grin, 'See what a little man-power does to you?'

She jerked the door open, but his voice stopped her retreat. 'Miss Jenner?' The words held an intimidating touch of authority. She waited. 'That money for your sister. It's a *gift*. Understand?'

Shelley tightened her lips, nodded and slammed the door behind her.

CHAPTER NINE

MURIEL ALLARD stayed away. Shelley found herself caught up in a whirlpool of work, unanswered queries, letters from educational administrators; commercial firms advertising their goods; letters from parents of pupils past, present and, it was hoped, future.

She was at her desk one morning when Craig walked in. Her elbow was resting on the hard wood of the surface, her hand was over her eyes. The fatigue she had felt the night before as she had sat in his mother's chair until gone ten o'clock had not left her.

Craig walked across to stand beside her. 'What's wrong?'

She lifted weary eyes and shrugged. 'Headache,' she lied, reaching for her spectacles which she had removed, but his hand stopped her. 'Look at me. White face, dark circles under the eyes ... Either you've been living it up with your boy-friend, or you're finding the strain of carrying the administration of this establishment too much for you. Which is it?'

Shelley was silent.

'Shelley,' he spoke quietly, 'I want the truth.'

She answered grudgingly. 'I haven't seen Emery for days. Janine's taken to treating him as her pet poodle and he goes wherever she beckons. That is,' her tired eyes lifted challengingly to his, 'when you're not occupying her time.'

'Jealous that your boy-friend's been snatched from you again by another woman?'

Something inside Shelley snapped. It must have been his mocking tone that did the damage. 'Damn my boy-friend!' she stormed. 'Damn you, damn all men ...' With startling suddenness she started crying.

Craig made no move to comfort her, he just stood there watching while she struggled with her tears. 'I'm sorry,' she murmured, blowing her nose, 'it's the tiredness.'

He went across to his mother's desk, sighed himself into

the chair and said, 'From now until my mother's return, just look on me as the man who shoulders the burdens. Come along, Miss Jenner. I'm in the hot seat now.' He indicated the piles of paper, neatly arranged but menacing in their quantity. 'Explain all this. I can see it's your handiwork by the incredible order and method. Any other woman carrying the weight of this place on her shoulders would be surrounded by chaos. But the intrepid Miss Shelley Jenner, with her passion for system and tidiness—an obsession which extends into her personal life—produces order from confusion at the touch of a button.' He watched as she pushed her handkerchief into her pocket and straightened her features in an expressionless composure.

He smiled mockingly. 'Maybe you're right. Maybe you are just an automaton with no feminine passions. I'll have to put your theory to the test some time.'

She walked stiffly across the room and pulled a chair beside him.

That evening, sitting in an armchair while Janine raced around upstairs dressing to go out, Shelley felt a weight had been lifted from her shoulders. Craig had taken over. She wished she could tell him how much his action of assuming authority had meant to her.

It was a joy to work for him. He was quick, precise, fluent in his dictation of letters, quite different from his mother's hesitating, meandering style, and without her time-wasting chatter. Yet it was a pain, too, to be so near to him, so in tune with his intellect, so intimate with his thoughts—those he allowed her to hear—and yet making contact with him in no other way.

He kept his distance. Their relationship was strictly impersonal, his manner businesslike and terse. There was nothing about him now of the mocking, lazy tormentor, a side which, even if it goaded her as it was intended to do, did not erect a barrier between them. On the contrary, it had, if anything, the effect of tearing it down.

Her eyes were closed, her mind dreaming when the knock had the door vibrating. There was a squeal from upstairs. 'Tell him I'm not ready,' Janine shouted.

Craig stepped in as Shelley opened the door. Janine, star-

140

ing down the stairs said, 'It's you! What have you come for? You're not taking me out tonight.'

Craig smiled up the stairs. 'It wouldn't be a bad idea,' he said, 'if you learnt a little tact from your elders.'

'If you mean me,' Shelley snapped, 'I'm not her mother, only her sister, I can't control how she behaves——'

His hand patting her shoulder had her jerking petulantly away. 'Calm down,' he said. 'Don't take everything so personally.' To Janine, 'I've come to see your sister, not you. And you can stop looking so worried. There's no more between Shelley and myself than between me and a deep freeze. At least, when the lid's open, a deep freeze allows the warmth to come flooding in!'

Janine laughed. 'She's not as cold as you think she is, Craig. Sometimes, when she was engaged, I'd go into the living-room when I thought it was empty and there was Shelley on the couch with Michael——'

'Jan!' Shelley shouted, desperate to put a stop to her sister's flow of words. Janine looked suitably contrite. 'Where are you going—the tennis club?'

Janine nodded. 'Emery's partnering me. Why?'

'Don't get back too late, will you?'

'Good God, woman,' Craig rasped, 'if the girl wanted to stay out all night you couldn't stop her.'

Shelley swung round. 'Will you mind your——'

'No, I won't.'

Janine laughed and came downstairs pulling on her jacket. 'I'll get myself out of here and leave you two to fight it out. Enjoy yourselves!' With a grin she waved and slammed the front door.

Craig gave Shelley his full attention. He looked her over with a kind of mocking relish and Shelley wished she had known he was coming. The cast-off dress of Janine's she was wearing was hardly one in which to entertain her employer's son. The dress had shrunk in the wash, noticeably so. It buttoned all the way down the front and there was a button or two missing at vital places. Craig's examining eyes overlooked nothing, certainly not the missing buttons, and Shelley tried self-consciously to draw together the edges which gaped open.

'So,' he said, sitting in the armchair opposite her, 'it's happened again. You've really let another woman take your man.'

Shelley sat, too, drawing up her bare feet—she had kicked off her sandals before Craig had arrived—and tucking them under her. 'What man?' she asked coldly.

'Emery Slade?'

She shook her head. 'Not "my man". Jan's welcome to him.' His unbelieving smile taunted her. 'And that's not sour grapes!'

'No?' He leaned forward, clasping his hands. 'Let me give you some advice. You've got as much as, if not more than any girl in your age bracket. Just use it in a certain way with the right man and he'd be yours to have and to hold. And,' softly, 'I mean "to hold". Make the first approach. It could be anything, a certain look, a hand on his hand, a smile that encourages him to approach you.'

Shelley responded bitterly, 'If all you've come to see me about is to give me avuncular advice on how to get my man——'

'*Avuncular* advice? So I'm behaving like an uncle now, am I?' He was out of the chair and standing over her. 'You make one more challenge to my virility, my girl, and you'll find yourself getting more—very much more—than you ever thought would come your way from a man.'

She coloured and her fingers moved agitatedly to where his eyes were resting—on the gap in the unbuttoned opening of her dress.

He stood for so long looking down at her that her cheeks grew warm. 'I'm sorry if you don't approve of what I'm wearing, but I wasn't expecting visitors.'

'Approve? My dear girl, the buttons—especially the missing ones—are an invitation in themselves. My fingers are itching to complete the striptease.' She looked up at him uncertainly, tremulously, and he smiled. 'I can't decide whether you're vibrating with fear or—hope?' He bent down and his hand reached out and settled round her throat. She sat rigid, helpless, filled with an overpowering longing. His fingers began to move, to stroke, to caress, and there was nothing she could do about it. There was not even the resistance in her to utter the single word 'stop'.

But he removed his hand and laughed as her head drooped with relief. 'You see,' he whispered, 'how vulnerable you are.' His expression changed and he walked away to stare out at the fir trees which lined the long drive to the house. He asked abruptly, 'When does the summer vacation begin?'

'Mid-July,' she muttered, struggling to recover from the touch of him. 'Ten more days, in fact. Are you——' She paused for courage because she was afraid to face the answer. 'Are you going back to the university? To your home?'

'Not until September.'

The relief that swept over her made her close her eyes. Two more months before he went away, two months of what? Heaven in seeing him almost every day? Misery in knowing the uselessness of her longing?

'This camping trip you're taking some of the kids on, is Slade going with you?'

'Emery? I think so. Why?'

'Has he been before?'

'No. It will be the first time for him as well as me.'

He turned in surprise. 'You've never been camping?'

'How could I? I've only worked for your mother since last October.'

'It seems longer. But I remember the woman before you. Now there was a dragon if there ever was one.' He strolled back to sit in the chair.

'Worse than me?' she smiled.

He returned her smile and Shelley's heart leapt. 'Much, much worse. She breathed smoke and fire. You only breathe smoke. I've learnt to fight my way through it—and survive.'

She asked, after a pause, 'Can I make you some coffee?'

'Thanks, no.' He looked at his watch and stood up. 'I'd like to stay, but I'm spending the evening with the Wallasey-Brownes.'

Shelley thought, standing unhappily to face him, only politeness stops him from saying 'with Sylva'.

'This outing with the boys,' Craig went on, 'how long

143

will it last?'

'Just under a week.'

'Presumably all the equipment's in good order?'

Shelley frowned. 'I hadn't thought about it. I'll have to ask Emery.'

'You will,' he mocked, 'certainly have to ask Emery. Otherwise you might find yourself sleeping under the stars instead of a tent.'

Shelley followed him to the door. She wished she could persuade him to stay, that she could behave with Janine's abandon and fling her arms round his neck, begging for a kiss, whispering to him, I'm lonely, keep me company, kiss me as Michael used to, only this time let it mean something instead of the pretence at loving that Michael indulged in . . .

'Shelley?' She did not realise Craig had been looking at her, studying her face. A hand tipped her chin. He whispered, his lips close to hers, 'You look so sad. Forget the past, sweet. We only have one life. Live it to the full before it's snatched away from you.'

She winced as if he had touched an open wound. He had, of course, because for the second time in her life her heart was slowly tearing itself apart. Tears flooded her eyes, she could not hold them back. She was in love with this man more deeply than she had ever believed it was possible to love. She had tried to protect herself, but until he had come smashing through her defences, she had not realised just how feeble they had been.

When his arms slipped round her she did not resist. When his hand strayed and found the gap in her dress she let it stay. The kiss he gave her had no meaning for him—wasn't he on his way to a date with the beautiful Sylva?—but to her, Shelley, it meant the whole world. He was not the marrying kind, he said. Yet for the second time in her life she had allowed a man to take her heart and grind it underfoot like a discarded cigarette.

When the kiss was over, he took a handkerchief from his pocket and dried her tears—tears which he thought were for another man.

Emery was hanging about the hall next morning waiting for

144

Shelley to arrive. He had, he said, come to see her about the camping marathon they were going on in ten days' time.

'The only consolation,' he said, 'is that I'm going with you.' He caught the hand that was about to place the spectacles on her nose and took them from her. 'Let's have a preview,' he said, 'of the degree of togetherness we can achieve when we get together in one of those ancient tents the staff are allocated.'

'You've had a look at the equipment?'

'Yes, and why the kids should get the new stuff and the staff the threadbare bits and pieces beats me. Come on, Shelley, it's about time you dropped this "touch me not" pose you've adopted towards me. A man like me has so much patience. Beyond that he's as lustful as any other male of the species.'

He started kissing her, and despite her protests that she should be working, and he should be teaching, that they could be interrupted at any moment, he would not stop. His kisses grew more insistent and, realising she could not fight him, Shelley went slack in his hold. 'That's better,' he murmured, and pursued his objective even more purposefully.

'Break down the touch barrier,' Craig had once urged her. 'Forget the past,' he'd said. 'You've only one life to live.'

No one came, the children were at their lesson and Emery grew more ardent. Shelley tried to convince herself it was only fair to him, she had held him off so long . . .

Footsteps, ringing and decisive on the parquet floor of the hall, stopped at the door. The handle turned. Craig Allard, the owner's son and at that moment every inch the acting head, came in.

Shelley and Emery broke apart, Shelley in confusion, Emery with a sheepish grin. Craig, his eyes slitted with anger, took in the situation. Then, with a sharp movement of his head, indicated the door. 'Out, Slade.'

Emery, in a weak gesture of defiance, raised his hand to Shelley. 'See you, darling,' he murmured, and went out.

Shelley, hoping fervently that the matter had ended with Emery's disappearance, pushed on her glasses. But if she

145

thought she had escaped castigation by the man who was currently in charge of the establishment, she was wrong.

'Hardly the time or the place for a necking session, Miss Jenner.' The caustic tone made her flinch. 'You don't get paid to let your boy-friend make love to you. If you haven't got enough work to keep you occupied, let me know. I can find plenty.'

The harshness, coming as it did after the gentleness and sympathy of the evening before, his sarcastic, grating phrases after the sweetness of his kiss, had her both on the defensive and the attack. Guilt added a rash asperity to her voice as she said, 'It was your fault. You told me last night it was time I gave a man the "come on" sign and let him get near me, so I took you at your word. Yet when I take your advice, all you can do is tell me off.'

'I'm delighted,' he said caustically, 'that you think well enough of me to take my advice on how to conduct your sex life. But as I said, you're paid to work, not to make love. Outside office hours and outside this building you can indulge your libido with as many men as you like, but from nine to five, excluding the lunch hour, the least you can do is to restrain your animal passions and get down to doing what you receive your salary for.'

Tears flooded her eyes, tears of anger at her inability to fight back. He was right, she had been in the wrong. Nor could Emery be accorded all the blame. If she had pushed him away as she should—and normally would—have done, he would have left her alone. But because with him, almost for the first time ever, she had let down her defences, he, man-like, had followed up his advantage.

But hadn't she only relaxed her vigilance because of what Craig had said last night? And hadn't she also wanted to prove to herself that she still had the ability to attract a man and make him *want* to make love to her? In other words, to regain a little of the self-confidence which had been so cruelly crushed by her fiancé's rejection?

She turned away, murmuring, 'I'm sorry. It won't happen again.'

He must have accepted her apology because a moment or two later he crossed to the desk and pulled a pile of documents towards him. There was silence for a while, with only the rhythmic clatter of the typewriter to disturb it. Then above it came Craig's voice asking her to stop. Shelley sat, hands in her lap, waiting for him to speak.

He said, glancing across the room, 'Since you're so inexperienced in the gentle art of camping, it would be in the best interests of everyone, especially the boys, if I were to go with you in place of Emery Slade. Send him a memo to that effect.'

Shelley took no pains to hide her anger. 'So you don't trust us! Just because you saw us kissing each other——'

His eyebrows lifted slowly, sardonically. 'My dear girl, a kiss is a mere nothing. If you'd only been kissing him—I'm no prude—I would have closed my eyes to it. But what you were engaged in could be described as a prologue to a much deeper relationship.'

'You're wrong,' she flared, 'you're deliberately exaggerating the situation, making what we were doing seem far worse than it really was. I told you he means nothing to me.'

'Which,' he responded cuttingly, 'puts you in a poor light indeed. If he is a man who means nothing to you, you were letting him go a long, long way. And, in my language, women who engage in that sort of activity coldly, deliberately, mechanically and without a vestige of feeling can only be described by one word, one that's not at all complimentary.'

'What,' she whispered, aghast, 'are you trying to say?'

He answered coolly, 'I should have thought it was perfectly obvious what I was trying to say.'

The blood ebbed from her cheeks, leaving her white as though she were ill. 'That's the grossest insult I've ever had flung at me! If you think I'm going to stay in the same room as you after that——' She rose and made for the door, but he was there before her, barring her way.

'Get back to your desk, please. We have work to do. Together. Unless,' an eyebrow lifted, 'you're resigning from your job?'

Slowly, defeatedly, choked with unhappiness, she returned to her seat. She stayed motionless for a few seconds while she tried valiantly to pull herself together, then, bracing herself, began to type the memo to Emery.

That day, thanks to Craig's financial backing, Janine was officially made a partner in Mrs. Caversham's hairdressing business. In the evening, Craig took her out to celebrate.

He wandered into the lodge and smiled a little derisively at the way Shelley was dressed. She was half reclining on the stairs, paintbrush in hand, staring down at him. There was no friendliness in her gaze. Her black, tight-fitting pants were stained with paint, her short green wrap-around overall likewise. Round her hair she had tied, peasant-style, a coloured square, and on her feet were tattered sandals.

'Not expecting a visit from our tame artist, that's for certain,' drawled Craig, leaning, hands in pockets, against the wall at the foot of the stairs. 'Bit late for spring-cleaning, isn't it?' he went on, in the same taunting tone. He tugged at his collar round which was tied a vivid, multi-coloured tie. 'Also, I'd say you were a little overdressed for this hot weather. Since you're not expecting visitors, I'd have thought you could have dispensed with some of those layers.'

Janine appeared at the top of the stairs. 'You should see what she's wearing—or rather, not wearing—under that overall!'

Shelley's head jerked up. 'Jan!' she reprimanded.

Craig murmured, amused, 'You're giving all her secrets away again, Jan, and Big Sister doesn't like it. So,' he said, contemplating Shelley's sprawling attitude over two or three stairs, 'she's cool, is she? Very cool indeed.'

Shelley flung back, 'As you said, I'm not expecting visitors, so I can dress——'

'Or undress,' Craig put in with a derisive grin.

'As I like.'

'Oh, stop it, you two!' Janine exclaimed. 'Why can't you be civilised and friendly for once? I've never heard anyone quarrel like you and Shelley, Craig, and over the silliest things, too!'

He watched Janine edge past her sister down the staircase. 'Maybe we're two silly people, Jan,' he murmured

148

with a smile.

Janine linked her arm in his. '*You're* not silly, Craig. Come on, we're going out to celebrate, so you'd better get in the right mood.' She threw a sisterly look at Shelley. 'Good thing you decided not to come with us. You and Craig would be scratching each other's eyes out the whole evening!'

Janine came in after midnight. She was bubbling over with slightly alcoholic joy. Or so Shelley thought as she eyed her climbing the stairs. 'For goodness' sake, Jan, mind the wet paint. You've had too much to drink. I should have told Craig——'

'Craig? It wasn't Craig. And anyway, you're wrong. I'm in love, Shelley. Oh,' she stretched luxuriously across Shelley's bed, 'it's a fabulous feeling.'

Shelley's heart lurched. So this was the end—of her dreams, her hopes, her future happiness? 'And Craig? Is he in love, too?'

Janine stared at her. 'Craig? Who said anything about Craig? The man I'm talking about's fabulous.' She laughed. 'I'm not as crazy as you think I am. I met him tonight. He's just brought me home.' She gave every sign of drifting into a dream world, so Shelley prodded her with her foot and Janine squealed, but it brought her to life.

'Craig took me to a place called the Broody Hen. Nothing broody about it. Bright lights, bars wherever you looked, dining, dancing. We were halfway through the meal when who should walk in but——'

'Sylva Wallasey-Browne?'

'Right first time.' Janine did not appear to notice the frown which corrugated her sister's forehead. 'She had one of those long embroided dresses on that you only see in the best shops. Her hair was out of this world, and of course she had a man beside her. She made straight for Craig, though, and he ordered the waiter to set the table for four.'

Shelley wondered dejectedly how long it would be before the announcement of Craig's and Sylva's engagement would appear in the newspapers.

'There we were,' Janine went on, 'Sylva eating Craig

149

with her eyes and me chewing over her partner. Wow! Has that man got everything—money, looks *and* a title. The Honourable Marius Halliday. I don't think Sylva can be serious about him, because we changed partners and Sylva went off with Craig, although how she could walk away and leave that fabulous man, I just can't guess. Shelley,' she gazed at her sister although not really seeing her, 'his car's an Aston Martin and he's just brought me home in it.'

'Well, I hope you thanked him nicely and said goodbye.' Shelley made her tone bracing. 'Because that's the last you'll see of him.'

'And that's where you're wrong, dear. He's taking me out tomorrow evening.'

Shelley frowned. 'Jan——'

'Little sister's grown up now, Shelley. She can run her own life without your well-meant but quite unnecessary help. And that doesn't mean I'm not grateful for all you've done for me.'

Shelley smiled weakly at her sister's unintentionally hurtful way of expressing her thanks. Then she remembered Craig's comments about Janine's ability to look after herself.

'But, Jan, don't be taken in by this man. He'll only be playing with you.'

'Will he, hell! I know a man who's really interested from one who's just passing the time. And Shelley,' her eyes were bright, 'I'm going to keep his interest.' She sat up and intoned dramatically, 'I'd love him even if he were out of work, penniless and homeless.'

'But he isn't, Jan...'

'No, he isn't, and isn't that just great!'

'Time,' said Shelley, looking at the clock on her bedside table, 'all good little girls were in bed.' A pause, then, 'Jan, you are a—good little girl?'

Janine gazed at her sister with absolute seriousness. 'Shelley darling, you have my word for it. I don't play around.'

Shelley was so relieved she could have cried. But all she said was, 'Good. Now I'm off to bed. Jan?' Janine looked up. 'I'm happy for you—about the partnership in the business, I mean.'

They laughed together and parted for the night.

Craig looked up briefly as Shelley walked into the office next morning. As she pushed her spectacles into place he leaned back in his chair and said,

'I've had another letter from my mother. She informs me that she and her major have talked over the possibility of their marrying each other and have come to the conclusion that it would be an admirable arrangement for both of them.' Craig leaned forward, elbows on desk. 'How would you like that, Miss Jenner? Coldbloodedly to consider marriage, no nonsense about love and involvement of feelings, just a business deal, a partnership, an "admirable arrangement." It should appeal to you.' His smile was mocking. 'Since you've once had your heart broken beyond repair— or so you allege—and consequently vowing never again to become entangled with another man, such a cool, level-headed liaison should commend itself to you wholeheartedly.'

Shelley answered slowly, 'I may have had my heart broken, but it hasn't left me heartless. I could never, ever, marry without love. I could never enter into an intimate relationship with a man for whom I had no feelings.'

'No? I don't believe you. I had the proof before my eyes yesterday morning in this room that you were capable of doing just that. Coldly and without an element of feeling, you were letting Emery Slade make ardent love to you and what's more, responding.'

'Can't you let the subject drop?' she cried. 'I told you, it was because of what you said about letting my barriers down. It was a—a kind of challenge. Michael Townley walked out on me. I leave you cold. At least Emery's shown interest ... I began to think there was something wrong with me. I was afraid——' Somehow she must stop herself pouring out her deepest fears. And the only way to do that was to remove herself from Craig's presence with all possible speed. She looked at her watch. It was a little early, but he would not know that.

She rose. 'If you'll excuse me, I have a reading class to

take. Mrs. Gordon's away again.' As she crossed the room he said, irritation sharpening his tone,

'Your place is here, not in front of a class. As I've said before, you're unqualified. Someone else must be found to replace Mrs. Gordon when she's off work—a trained teacher.'

Shelley replied defiantly, 'Your mother has no objection to my doing it. In fact she encourages me.'

'Of course she does. Because it saves her money. If you didn't do it, she would have to employ a qualified part-time teacher, whereas you, like a fool, do the job uncomplainingly for the mere pittance she gives you as her secretary.'

Shelley grew agitated. Now it really was time for her to go. 'I'm sorry, the class will be waiting...' She cut the sentence short and ran. If she had stayed to finish it she knew he would have taken active steps to prevent her going, even restraining her physically. And these days she would rather risk Craig Allard's displeasure than the touch of his hands.

Janine went out with the Hon. Marius Halliday and returned bright-eyed and loquacious. It seemed they had driven on to the moors, parked the car and spent most of the time talking. Although what a newly qualified young hairdresser and a rich, fast-living young member of the aristocracy had in common sufficiently to spend hours discussing it, Shelley could not imagine.

The situation worried her a little, but she reasoned that provided Janine did not take the young man seriously, the experience of being taken around by such a person could do her no harm and might even do some good.

It seemed that Janine's friendship with Craig had come to an abrupt end. Shelley supposed that Sylva was in favour again. How long would it be before he succumbed to her attractions, forfeited his bachelor freedom and became 'the marrying kind?'

Emery took the dispensing of his services as one of the leaders of the camping holiday at first with resentment and annoyance, then with resignation. Two days before the start of the trip Craig called at the lodge, meeting Janine in the hall. But she dashed past him to join Marius Halliday as he screeched to a stop outside the front door.

When she had gone, Craig asked, 'How do you like your sister dallying with an offshoot of the British aristocracy? Haven't you tried putting pressure on her to give up her association with her rich playboy?'

Shelley shrugged. 'As long as she doesn't get serious about him, I don't object. Why should I? And even if I did, what good would it do? As you keep telling me, I'm not my sister's keeper. She's nearly twenty, after all.'

'You're not afraid she'll get too—involved?'

Shelley frowned. 'If you mean what I think you mean, then surely you're a better judge of that possibility than I am? You've taken her around for some while, long enough to test her powers of refusal.' She smiled and her eyebrows arched, asking him a silent question.

'If that remark was intended to get out of me how far I personally went with her, then all I can say is, "I pass".'

Shelley said, her face wooden, 'Why did you come?'

'Not for the welcome I knew I'd get from you.'

'I'm sorry. If you'd given me advance warning, I'd have put down the red carpet and mustered a reception committee, not to mention dressed in my best.'

He plainly took objection to her sarcasm because his eyes flickered with a passing but intense anger, but it was under control within seconds. Instead it turned into a cool appraisal of her clothes, the black low-cut top with its scarlet appliquéd flowers across the front, and the scarlet trousers, both of which she had borrowed from Janine, at Janine's insistence. Janine had styled her hair again, and it hung in softly curling layers to her shoulders.

Craig, however, made no comment. His eyes were unreadable, too, and Shelley felt fiercely self-conscious, wishing for a moment that she was hiding as usual behind the dull façade of her working clothes.

Craig walked away to stare out of the window. Shelley sat curled up in her chair, watching the rigidity of his back and sensing that something was troubling him. When he turned, he was serious and withdrawn.

'I came to see you,' he said, 'because I had a phone call

153

from my mother this evening. She's on her way across Europe and is apparently making for Scandinavia. She's not alone on her travels this time.' He paused and looked at her, a deep frown drawing his brows together. 'It seems I now have a stepfather.'

Shelley uncurled her legs and, with an immense effort, pulled herself from the chair. She felt like a man who had detected an earth tremor beneath his feet and knew it was only the beginning and that the earthquake proper, the havoc, the devastation, was yet to come.

The announcement winded her, drained her of colour and, momentarily, of life. 'You mean,' she whispered, 'your mother has married again?'

'What else could I mean? My stepfather's name, apparently, is Major Hunter, Major Eric Hunter.' Craig gave a twisted smile. 'In view of my age in relation to his, he has invited me to call him Eric.'

'But—but when did it happen?'

'The wedding? A few days ago. They wanted no fuss, no presents, no relatives, not even me, the bride's son. Not even, apparently, the daughter the bridegroom had by his first wife. The young woman, they tell me, is only a year or two younger than I am. My mother and stepfather are honeymooning now.'

'But,' Shelley ran her tongue over her lips, 'the school?' She motioned with her hand in the direction of the house. 'What's going to happen to all that?'

He said, his eyes blank, 'I have more news for you. Since it seems they don't intend to settle down anywhere at present—apparently my stepfather shares my mother's roaming instincts, which is just as well—my mother has given me—I repeat, *given* me—Mapleleaf House School. Since the building is already my property, she says, all it contains, the kids, the equipment, the problems, should also be mine. So,' with a brief, exasperated sigh, 'she's left the baby well and truly on my doorstep.'

'What will you do, Craig?'

'Do?' He lifted a shoulder noncommittally. 'It's anybody's guess. I've hardly had time to consider the position. It's only,' he consulted his watch, 'twelve minutes since I put the receiver down after speaking to her.'

So he had come at once to tell her? That, Shelley felt, at least was something to treasure, she had his confidence to that extent. But of course he would have to tell his mother's secretary, wouldn't he? After all, she dealt with the head teacher's correspondence, both private and general.

'But, Craig, your job——?'

'At the university?' He turned to the window again and for a long time studied the gravel outside the window, although it was plain he was not seeing a single pebble. Then he said at last, 'That is my true vocation. By instinct I'm a teacher, but not of children, otherwise I would have become a schoolteacher. As I've told you before, kids *en masse* just don't appeal. By training and inclination I'm a teacher of adults.'

'But, Craig,' there was a waver in her voice and he turned to look at her, 'the school—what about the school? If you reject it, what will happen to it—to the children, the staff and—and me?'

CHAPTER TEN

For long time Craig did not reply to the question. And even when he did, he answered indirectly.

'One thing I can say for certain. I'm not taking my mother's place. You know my views on privately-run educational establishments. Also there are a lot of things wrong with the place. Everything is too traditional—the teaching methods, the outlook of the staff. The science equipment needs renewing, the classes are too large for a fee-paying school.'

'You could bring in a new head teacher,' Shelley suggested.

He looked at her speculatively. 'You favour my allowing the school to continue?'

Shelley studied her hands. 'Don't ask me. I'm hardly a disinterested onlooker. My job's tied up with the place. And,' she found some courage to look at him, 'my home.'

He strolled across to stand in front of her and looked for some time into her wavering, troubled eyes. She could not stand the intensity of his gaze, yet she could not tear her eyes from his.

'Craig——?' she whispered uncertainly. If she stretched out her hand and grasped his arm, if she pleaded, 'Don't go away, don't go back to your job, stay here and run the school as your mother did and I would work for you to the end of my days,' would he relent and agree? But she knew that trying to persuade him to change the course of his career at this stage in his life would be like trying to coax a mountain to move.

But, her mind persisted, if she whispered, 'Don't leave me. I love you and can't imagine life without you', what would he do then?

At last he moved away. Whatever he had seen in her eyes had obviously left him unimpressed.

'I shall have to give the matter a great deal of thought.'

At the door he turned. 'How many children are coming on this trek into the great unknown?' Six, she told him. 'I take it everything's ready—equipment, food and so on?'

Everything was ready, she said. 'We leave on Friday morning in the minibus.'

'Destination?'

She gestured vaguely. 'The moors. Not too far away. It's just to keep them occupied until their parents come for them.'

Craig nodded and with a brief goodnight, he left her.

When Janine came home, the news about Craig's mother surprised but did not shatter her. She was wrapped about in a blanket of happiness.

'Marius is a darling,' she sighed. 'He said he's serious about me. He said I'm just what he's been looking for.'

Shelley frowned and remarked, in an attempt to bring her sister back to earth, 'I suppose you know we're in danger of losing the roof over our heads?'

Janine said, 'So what? Marius won't let us roam the streets homeless.'

It was impossible to get through to her, so Shelley prepared herself to listen until bedtime to the eulogies that poured from her sister's lips about the man she seemed quite seriously to have fallen in love with. The faintest stirrings of hope that Janine's feelings might be reciprocated were beginning to register in Shelley's brain. If Marius Halliday was as serious about Janine as she seemed to be about him, then at least one problem would have been lifted from Shelley's shoulders.

It was the afternoon of the third day of camp. The weather had, so far, been unbelievably kind. Shelley was sitting, knees drawn up, watching the boys play cricket.

She was wearing a skirt and a sleeveless top and she looked at her arms with their deep tan and her bare legs which, although paler, because she had mostly worn trousers, had likewise reacted to the sun's rays.

Her eyes wandered about the landscape. Although the hills barely topped fifteen hundred feet, they rose so abruptly from the fields and meadows that their height appeared much greater than it really was. Cliffland or Cleveland, the first Scandinavian settlers had named it. As they had gone for walks, Craig had pointed here and there to evidence of occupation by prehistoric man. There were burial mounds, earthworks, even foundations of huts.

Craig ... Shelley's eyes shifted to glance covertly at the reclining figure of the man a short distance away, resting on his elbow, reading. When they had not been walking with the boys, or cooking the meals and doing the other jobs connected with keeping six hungry, energetic specimens of young manhood well fed and happy, Craig had spent his spare time reading. And reading and reading ...

She dragged her eyes away—they returned to his recumbent form again and again, but he seemed entirely unaware of the fact—and let them roam the countryside. From the height at which they had set up camp, she could see here and there farmhouses, grey-walled and built of local stone, with no visible road leading to them, only well-worn tracks.

Remote and lonely—the word applied to herself as well as to those old farms. They were as isolated as she was, cut off from most modern forms of communication just as she was cut off from Craig. It was he who had effected the 'disconnection'. He treated her politely but distantly, although to the boys he was friendliness itself.

There was a pain inside her that the peace all round, the sight of quiet, undemanding sheep grazing along the unfenced roads, the sighing of the wind through the grasses and heather, could not salve. Surely, she tortured herself, he would have behaved in a much more friendly way to any other person who had accompanied him, whether they had been male or female? Could it, she asked herself, be just because my name's Shelley Jenner, and he must not under any circumstances let me begin to think I mean more to him than any other member of the school's staff? Or any other of the women he has known and no doubt, in passing, made love to in the course of his thirty odd years?

Her head swivelled towards him again, this time involuntarily, and she found he was looking at her. Her heart pumped furiously and the look she returned was unintentionally belligerent. How could she help it when he was hurting her so much?

The cries and shouts of the boys vied with the call of the curlews and the circling birds to disturb the air. A plane droned aimlessly across the endless sky, an insect buzzed near Shelley's ear and she jerked her head to make it go away.

Then, tired of the ache which had her in its grip, she lay back and felt the rough grass scratch her neck. Irritably she sat up and saw that Craig was moving towards her. His shirt was undone, revealing his chest which was deeply tanned. His trousers were light-coloured and well-fitting.

'Trouble?' he asked, his mouth curving into a slight smile.

'Can't get comfortable,' she replied shortly. He was aware of her presence at last, but paradoxically it seemed to increase her irritability.

He said, 'I suggest something to rest your head on. I'll play Sir Galahad for once and find you a pillow. Any objections if I invade the privacy of your tent?'

It would be the first time since we arrived, she thought a little sourly, but shook her head. He bent down to let himself under the flap. He emerged with an inflated cushion and said, 'Try that.'

He waited until she had lowered herself into a reclining position, then he lifted her head, his fingers sinking into her hair, and pushed the cushion under it.

The touch of him brought the colour surging into her cheeks. In an effort to hide it, she turned on her side away from him, and said, in a brittle voice, 'Thank you very much.'

'Don't mention it.' He seemed to be smiling. Then he went on, standing beside her, 'It's a good thing the weather's behaved. With those two tents you and I are sleeping in, even a few showers could have brought disaster. Trust my mother to order the new equipment for the fee-paying toddlers, and forget to do likewise for the teachers. If I'd known the two staff tents hadn't been renewed for an unknown number of years, I'd have called the whole thing off.'

He sat beside her. If he had wanted, he could have touched her, but the fact that he had no intention of doing

159

so became clear in the first few seconds.

Shelley opened her eyes, twisted round and saw that he was gazing around as she had been doing, drinking in the beauties of the moors and hills. Nearby a stream flowed and frothed over smooth, time-worn stones. A fight threatened to break out between two of the boys and Craig's muscles tensed, ready to intervene, but the quarrel ended as abruptly as it had started.

Shelley's despair grew with the long silence. Had they lost all means of communicating with each other? Now and then there was a whirr of grouse rising unexpectedly into the air; or a sheep bleated in answer to another.

With her head resting on her linked hands, Shelley studied Craig's profile. It was impassive and remote, his eyes narrowed slightly against the brightness of the sun. He must have felt her regard because his head turned slowly. She did not move her eyes—she could not, it was beyond her power.

Their gaze clashed and held fast, like a well-knotted rope having an interminable strain imposed on it. It was like a game of tug-of-war. Shelley, her body vibrating with a primitive longing, felt her will-power slipping slowly away, and was the first to yield and concede victory.

Warmth enveloped her, of embarrassment, confusion— and humiliation. Because he did not move a muscle to follow up his victory. He must have known, he must have *felt* her response to the look they had exchanged. Man that he was, he must have guessed her feelings, her needs, the unbearable desire he had, by that narrow, assessing look, aroused in her.

But he merely turned his head towards the boys. Moments later he joined them.

It was evening and the boys had settled down to sleep. Shelley was scanning the sky and noting, for the first time since they had left home, that clouds were forming over the hills. They did not look ominous, so she was not worried.

She had changed after tea into trousers and long-sleeved white top. It would be pleasant, she decided, to go for a walk. She had to do something to fill in the lonely evening.

160

There had been no sign of Craig for some time and she assumed he was reading or writing in his tent. She glanced in that direction and saw that he was standing outside it. He had changed, too, into a roll-necked navy shirt and trousers. He made a splash like spilt ink against the once-white canvas of the tent.

His thumbs were hooked over his belt and he was looking her over lazily. 'Going for a walk?' he asked. As she nodded and turned to go, he joined her without invitation.

So her bid for freedom from heartache had been thwarted. The cause of it was going with her. She was glad they could not venture far from the children and that their shared walk would consequently be a short one.

They were silent and Shelley wished she could find a way of breaking it. A sideways glance at his profile told her nothing. She hazarded, 'Craig? What are you going to do about the school?'

They had walked a good number of paces before he answered. 'I've been doing a great deal of thinking this last day r so.' Another long pause, with only the sound of their shoes brushing against the grasses to break it. 'As yet I've reached no decision.'

'Will you consult your mother first?'

'No, why should I? She's given me the school, put the whole damned lot on my plate.'

'Would your——' she looked up at him, 'would your stepfather be able to advise?'

'I don't need advice.'

Colour crept up her neck and over her cheeks at his terseness. 'I'm sorry.'

'Talking of my stepfather,' he spoke slowly and there was a hint of a smile on his face, 'he has a daughter. I told you that, didn't I?' Shelley glanced at him again, wondering what was coming. 'But I didn't tell you that in the course of my conversation with my mother she told me she was looking forward to my meeting her new stepdaughter. Myra's the name.' He looked down at Shelley reflectively, and still there was that odd ghost of a smile. Was the turmoil she was experiencing, Shelley wondered, showing in her eyes?

161

'According to my mother, Myra's just right for me. She's —let me try to remember the exact words. She's sweet, placid, has all the social graces and is decorative into the bargain. Academically, it seems, she's not too bright, but as my mother reminded me, I never did admire intelligent women.' Now the smile was tinged with malice. 'What do you think? Should I take myself a wife, especially one with all those admirable qualities. I must admit I'm getting bored with being a bachelor.'

His tone betrayed that he intended to goad and goaded Shelley was. She stood in his path and faced him squarely. 'Sweet, placid, malleable, decorative—what more could you want? And dim-witted into the bargain. Yes, marry the girl. Although you swear you're not the marrying kind, tie yourself to a lifeless, dumb, good-to-look-at socialite and spend the rest of your life regretting it. It's no more than you deserve!' she flung at him, and turned and raced back to the camp, leaving him looking after her.

Shelley remained in her tent until she heard Craig go into his, then she gathered her towel, soap and flannel and crept down to the stream. It was dusk. The sun had gone below the cloud-laden horizon. There was a chill in the air, but it did not deter Shelley from taking off her white top. She knelt beside the stream and revelled in the soft, cool water, washing her arms, neck and face.

She towelled herself, feeling with pleasure the glow the rough surface of the towel left behind. Something, it might have been a pebble disturbed or the brisk chafe of heather against shoe, made her tense. Over her shoulder she saw that Craig, hands in pockets, was watching her.

She sat back on her heels. 'Please go away,' she said, but he did not move.

'Why?' was his cool reply. 'A man may look at a beautiful woman. I'm not touching you.'

But he was, with his eyes. She could almost feel them. I'm not a child, she told herself. I'm no coy young girl. I've been on the brink of marriage. So she forced herself to tolerate his gaze. She stood, preparing to make her way back to the tent. Because of the slope of the land upwards from the stream, she had to move along the path towards him.

As she approached he deliberately blocked the way. 'Please,' she whispered, 'let me pass.'

'Give me one good reason why I should.'

Panic rose, shortening her breath and tightening her muscles. For the second time that day she could not tear her eyes from his. Her belongings were clutched to her, but one by one he took them from her, dropping them to the ground. Wildly she looked round.

'There's no one about, my sweet,' he murmured, 'not a single soul. All the boys are sleeping. I've checked.' Then his arms were about her, his mouth over hers. His hands were moving across her shoulders, running down her arms, finding the bareness of the soft flesh around her waist. Kiss followed kiss and she could do nothing but cling and respond and meet his ardour.

Myra ... Or it might have been *Sylva*. Or *Janine*. All the women in his life, and who knew how many more? The words drifted about her mind like seeds blown by the breeze, but her mind was dulled by the joy of his touch and the hard reality of his body against hers.

Myra ... *Shall I marry her?* he'd asked. *I'm growing bored with bachelorhood.*

So the last few days he'd been bored, perhaps, with Shelley Jenner's company, her quietness, her intelligence which he so despised?

With an energy born of desperation, she began to struggle and to fight him off. She succeeded in freeing her mouth from his ardent lips and pressed her head away from him. 'What's the matter?' she cried. 'Are you missing the charms of your other lady friends so much that you're using me, the only woman in sight, to fill the gap they've left in your *bachelor* life?'

He drew a sharp breath and his fingers bruised as he took her more securely into his hold. 'You're no prude,' he said. 'That much I know from the things your sister's let drop about you. You know as well as I do this little interlude hasn't been a one-sided affair. Why don't you admit that I attract you as a man as much as you attract me as a woman? Your eyes are loaded with desire, I can see that every

163

time I look at you. So stop accusing me of making all the running. Whenever I've kissed you, you've responded like a woman who's wanted more—and more.'

The truths he was flinging at her had her twisting with humiliation inside and with indignant strength against the circle of his arms.

'All right,' he muttered, his eyes brilliantly angry against the darkening sky, 'if that's what you want . . .'

He gripped her agonisingly for a few seconds more, then thrust her away and she crumpled on to the heather. He left her slumped there with her face in her hands, and went inside his tent, securing the flap.

It was the noise that woke her, the howling of the wind across the moors, the straining and dragging of the tent against the guy ropes, the hiss of the gale through grass and heather. And the pelting of the rain on the canvas, the worn, torn and in places tattered canvas, which had stood the test of so many years, but which because it was intended only for the staff had been overlooked by Mrs. Allard when she had ordered new camping equipment.

Shelley felt the steady, heavy drip on her forehead as she stirred uneasily and opened her eyes. It was pitch dark, but when she switched on her torch, she wished she hadn't. Above her head was a tear through which the rain was steadily penetrating. Near to it was a hole through which it was possible to see the blackness outside. The edges of the canvas were flapping and the ropes were groaning against the pegs which struggled to hold them down.

The boys! She must go across and see them. They might be scared or shouting, and if they were it would be impossible to hear them over the whine of the wind and the drumming of the rain.

She sat up—too quickly, because her head hit the canvas and released a deluge all over her hair, face and neck. The tear above her had widened and water was pouring through. Other holes appeared and now rain was flinging itself underneath the tent. A few more minutes and she would be flooded out.

Her torch flickered—it needed a new battery—but she

164

groped about and found her coat. It was saturated with water. Her pile of clothes, pitiful in the dim light, had suffered a similar fate. The tent stretched and strained, ballooning out and caving in, and all the time there was the roaring fury of the wild elements outside in the darkness.

At the moment the tent collapsed, Shelley heard Craig shouting. But she could not answer because there was a suffocating darkness all round her, and she fought to escape from the massive enveloping weight which pulled her to the ground which was itself squelching and sodden under her hands and knees.

She shrieked in sheer terror, fighting for breath and freedom from the claustrophobia which had her in its grip. Her name was being called, over and over again and over the howling of the wind. Hands were tearing at the canvas, pulling, lifting and after a millennium of time, penetrating the soaking shroud.

In moments she was freed and being carried through the storm to dryness, safety and sudden peace.

'The boys,' she gasped, 'the boys . . .'

'Sound asleep,' was the terse answer. 'Tents as firm as rocks.' She was lowered on to something soft and warm. 'Who put up your tent?'

'The boys,' she murmured. 'They asked if they could and I let them.'

'I might have known! The pegs were pushed in, not hammered. The guy ropes were twisted round them like cotton and left unsecured.'

'It wasn't only that,' she murmured, near to tears at his tone. 'It was the holes——'

'You needn't tell me—I know. Thanks to my mother's gross negligence . . .'

A towel was thrust into her hand. 'Dry yourself. You'll have to take off those clothes. I'll lend you a sweater.'

She shook her head like a drunken man. 'It doesn't matter.'

'You're not catching pneumonia, girl. I've enough on my hands without that.' He watched as she wiped the rain from her face.

'Your hair—here, give me that towel.' He rubbed until

165

she cried out to him to stop.

'Th-there's no need t-to be so rough . . .'

He heard the quiver in her voice and stopped at once, flinging down the towel and standing near the entrance. When she was ready to remove her wet clothing he pulled up the hood of the anorak he was wearing and said he would see how many of her belongings he could recover from the debris.

By the time he returned she had struggled into his sweater and a pair of trousers he had taken from his rucksack. In his arms was a bundle of clothes and other belongings. These he dumped in a pile beside her.

Shelley thanked him and started shivering. From somewhere he produced a vacuum flask and poured a cup of steaming milk. 'I'd prepared it in case of emergencies. But at this moment you're in greater need than the boys.'

Her palms handled the mug lovingly, not shrinking from the burning heat. The liquid ran over her tongue and down her throat, ending her shaking and filling her with warmth. As she handed back the mug, thanking him, Craig poured a little more milk into it and tipped it down his throat, afterwards putting the flask away.

'What's the time, Craig?' she whispered.

He shone the torch on his watch. 'One o'clock.' He looked down at her. 'Somehow we have to sleep. Your sleeping bag's as wet as a sponge.' He smiled, but his eyes stayed cool. 'You'll have to move over, won't you?'

His sleeping bag was underneath her and she looked up, unbelievingly. 'You don't mean——?'

'I do.'

'That we *share* it?'

'Why not?'

'But we can't, we *can't* . . .'

He unzipped his anorak and threw it down. Shelley struggled to get away from the sleeping bag. 'I'll sit up all night, Craig, I don't mind. Here,' she took a handful of bag and offered it to him, 'have it. It's yours. I'm not sharing it with you. I'd rather——'

'Exactly what do you think I have in mind?' The tone was biting, the lips that mouthed the words tight and furious. 'Don't tell me, I know. But let me tell *you* something. I've got to be *attracted* to a woman before I can even begin to *think* in those terms, let alone anything else.'

She could hardly speak for pain—the pain of rejection which fixed her like a revolver shot straight at her heart. But she managed to say, through trembling lips, 'This evening, you—you kissed me...'

'What's a kiss?' he tossed at her cynically. 'You surely aren't equating a meeting of the lips with a meeting of the——'

She clapped her hands over her ears. 'Stop insulting me, for pity's sake!' Her head rested on her bent knees. 'You've said enough...' Her body shuddered as her mind absorbed the full meaning of his words. Her lips were stiff as she muttered, 'You'll have to share the sleeping bag, won't you? Since you hate me so much, I'll be safe, quite, quite safe...' Her voice faded away.

'No, thanks.' He lowered himself to the ground, which was covered by a waterproof sheet. 'I've changed my mind. Keep the bag. I'll sleep here.'

'But it's cold, bitterly cold.' She gestured to the flapping, sucked-out sides of the tent.

'I'll survive.' He lay full length and turned his back to her.

She had no option but to slide down into the quilted warmth of the bag and lie still. She must have slept, but only fitfully, because when she woke only an hour had passed. In the intermittent lulls in the relentless battering of the storm, she heard the deep breathing of her companion. Cautiously she reached out for his torch and switched it on, covering the light with outspread fingers.

He was lying half on his side, quite without covering. It would be terrible to leave him exposed like that all night. The least he would catch, she argued with herself, was a cold, and probably worse. Her conscience, no, her *love* would not let her rest until she had provided him with some kind of cover.

There was only one thing she could do. Firmly she put aside propriety, shyness and constraint. Strange how, once her mind had surmounted the obstacles, it was so easy for her actions to follow. She scrambled out of the sleeping bag, unzipped it and opened it out until it became a double-sized quilt.

In a few moments she was beside Craig and the cover was over both of them. Her warmth must have reached out to him because he stirred slightly and turned, although she knew instinctively he was still asleep. His proximity was more potent than she had in her wildest moments even dreamed. She started shaking again, but trying desperately to contain her shudders so as not to bring him to full consciousness.

It was no use. With an almost compulsive movement—as though it was a primitive impulse outside his control—he took her into his arms.

The shudders persisted and now his whole body was shielding her, willing her to be still. His palm stroked her hair, pressed her face to his chest. A hand ran down her body, as if by the contact it would bring the shaking to an end. But to her dismay it increased. So bitter-sweet was his touch, the hardness of his limbs, his chest against which her cheek nestled, she was coming to glowing life within his hold.

'Be still, girl,' he whispered harshly, 'be still, for God's sake.' Then he groaned and it was as if something within him snapped and his mouth sought hers with an urgency which caught her up in its tide. She was swept along, almost going under, and like a drowning person, pictures passed through her mind—of his kisses on the edge of the sea, after the dance, by the stream that evening ... Waves bore down upon her, lifting her high, letting her go, lifting her again, only to break over her head.

'Craig, please,' she begged against his lips, '*please ...*'

She must not drown in the whirlpool of his desires ... At last she began, feebly at first, then with every muscle in her body, to struggle against the treacherous currents. Now she knew the imperative need for self-control, the absolute necessity for stillness and tranquillity.

He was a man, and with every fibre of his body he was reacting to the feel of a woman in his arms. It was not her, Shelley, he was responding to, but merely the fact that she was female. Didn't she know just what he thought of her?

168

Hadn't he told her so only this evening? Brutally, frankly he had let her know in so many ways. In these intimate circumstances any woman would have had the same effect on the masculinity in him...

The thought saddened and sobered her and she began the fight to force herself to resist his demands and grope her way back to sanity. It was the way her body stiffened and drew away that must have told him what she was attempting to do.

'All right,' he said, in a rough, brittle voice. 'I get the message. You can't stand my touch. Maybe it reminds you of the man you were going to marry. You probably still love him and any other man's lovemaking repels you. But, my God, you asked for it, putting yourself beside me...'

She began to cry. Was that what he thought of her, that she was wanton? 'It's not that at all,' she sobbed, 'I only wanted to help you——'

It was the wrong word and of course he made the most of it. '*Help* me? You couldn't have chosen a better way.' The voice was dry. 'Now come on, relax.' More softly, 'Relax, Shelley. You're safe from me. I won't violate you, girl. I'm in control.'

Yes, she thought bitterly, you're in control now you're fully conscious and aware of who I am, of my lack of attraction... But she grew quiet and allowed her muscles slowly to lose their tension.

'Turn around,' he murmured, helping her with strong, firm hands, 'and sleep.'

In this at least she desired to please him, so she did as he commanded and, in his quiet arms, she slept.

Through the mists of her dream drifted words. 'My sweet, my sweet one...' Arms held her securely. Only half awake herself, Shelley realised Craig was dreaming, too. He was talking, in that dream, to one of his women friends.

Sylva, Janine, Myra. Sylva, Janine, Myra... The names went on and on in her confused mind. He thinks I'm one of those. It's not me he's dreaming about. I don't even *attract* him.

Shelley stirred and the arms about her tightened, so she

169

lay still. She must not disturb him from his dreams. Easily, happily, she slipped down into a dream of her own. She was lying beside the man she loved. He loved her, she was his and he was hers . . .

When she opened her eyes again, it was daylight. Carefully she moved away from the arms which were lying loosely around her. Craig remained still, so it seemed she had not disturbed him. Outside the wind persisted but had muted overnight to a strong breeze. Nor was there any sound of rain. But when Shelley pushed the hair from her eyes and lifted the flap to peer out, there was a veiled dampness everywhere, in the sky, over the hills and heather, in the rain-swollen clouds which hung so low they enveloped the landscape in a humid mist.

In the semi-darkness of the tent, she groped for her compact and propped it open on the floor. Then she knelt and with a comb pulled at the tangles in her hair. Something made her look in Craig's direction.

He was lying on his back, hands supporting his head, the cover still over his legs. His mouth was lifted in a sardonic smile as he watched her.

'Repairing the ravages of the night?' She did not respond. 'So you slept with me after all?'

The words, taunting, tormenting, had the colour flooding her face. Gone was his gentleness, the passion that in its ferocity had vied with the raging storm outside. Only cynicism was left, as stark and painful as an uprooted tree.

'I—I didn't think you'd remember.'

He turned on to his side, propping his head with his hand. He seemed prepared to enjoy the next few minutes. 'You can't mean it? You didn't really think you could put yourself beside a man in the night without his being fully aware of it—and *remembering*?' She had nothing to say. 'I believe you said you did it to *help* me?' He smiled, but it did not warm his eyes. 'It must have cost you a great deal, that Good Samaritan act. You with your hatred of the male sex!'

'I—I couldn't lie there warm and comfortable in your sleeping bag while you had no covers over you.'

'So it was guilt feelings that motivated you?'

170

'What else?' she blurted out, deeply hurt by his insinuation that her unselfish action was merely the prodding of her conscience. 'You didn't think I did it for *love*, did you?'

'Love?' he said softly. 'My dear Shelley, I know for certain now that you don't know the meaning of the word.'

She rounded on him. If I don't, she wanted to cry, what is this feeling I have for you? But she said, 'I've been engaged. I've been on the brink of marriage. I loved—I——' she hesitated and bit back the words 'I thought I loved.' 'So how can you say I don't know what love means?'

His only reply was a deepening of his taunting smile.

'You might thank me,' she said, 'for what I did.'

'For the great and noble sacrifice you made on my behalf?' He sketched a mocking bow with his arm and head. 'Please accept my lifelong gratitude for so valiantly putting your virtue into jeopardy by sleeping with me and giving me half share of your cover.'

'Can't you even be sincere and pleasant when you're *thanking* me?' she cried, stung by his mockery.

He looked her over with amusement. 'It's too early in the morning to be angry,' he drawled. 'Although I must admit it enhances your looks. With that black hair in a tangle, your eyes blazing and the colour glowing in your cheeks, you make a man want to reach out,' he followed the words with the action, 'and grab you.'

She evaded the clutching hand and dived for the open door. There was shouting and laughter coming from the boys' tents.

Shelley wandered across to the wreck in which she had been trapped and contemplated it ruefully. Underneath the soaking fabric her belongings looked pitiful. They lay in a pile on the squelching ground—clothes, toilet articles, rucksack. She wondered if they would ever recover from their drenching.

Craig joined her, pulling on his anorak. 'Well, we have a choice to make. Either we go home today or,' he eyed her with a smile, 'you spend the rest of the day in my sweater and trousers, like a sheep in wolf's clothing, and in addition, you spend another night sleeping with me.' He low-

171

ered his voice. 'The only trouble is, I couldn't give you a guarantee of restraint on my part for two nights running. It would be imposing an impossible strain on my male reflexes.'

She said sharply, 'I thought I didn't even begin to attract you in that way?'

'My dear girl, as was so clearly demonstrated in the early hours of this morning, in the blackness of the night "attraction" doesn't matter greatly to a man when there's a woman lying beside him.'

She fought the lump in her throat and turned away so that he would not see the sudden tears of humiliation, the expression of total failure on her face. She snapped, 'We go home.'

He laughed softly. 'Yes, I thought the idea of spending another night with me would repel you.'

'What you've been saying,' she returned defensively, 'merely bears out my already low opinion of men in general.'

'And me in particular?'

She swung away, making for the boys' tents. Craig followed. Shelley had an uproarious welcome. She had forgotten how odd she must look in her borrowed clothes, and the boys' laughter made her wonder just how she looked to Craig. When she explained what had happened to her tent in the night, how it had fallen on top of her and Mr. Allard had dragged her from under it, the boys rolled on the ground, helpless with laughter.

But when Craig explained to them that because Miss Jenner now had no tent of her own, they had no alternative but to break camp and return home, there were groans and pleadings and various ingenious ideas for overcoming the obstacle. Craig was adamant, however, saying that Miss Jenner agreed with him, after which the boys accepted the decision and packed their belongings.

After breakfast, which Shelley prepared with the aid of a Primus stove, they drove back to Mapleleaf House under leaden skies. The boys' spirits were high and so, oddly, were Craig's. As he drove, he talked to the boys about the history and geology of the Cleveland Hills. He spoke simply so that they could understand and answered their questions patiently and knowledgeably, holding their attention until they were nearly home.

'I thought you said,' Shelley commented, as they turned into the drive leading to the house, 'you were not a teacher of children, but only of adults?'

He pulled up with a jerk outside the lodge, and the boys fell against each other, shrieking with laughter. Craig's eyebrows lifted at her question. 'You think I'm wrong? You think I could apply for a job as a teacher in what is now my own school?'

The question, phrased as it was, raised her hopes sky high. Her heart beat quickly as she asked, staring through the windscreen, 'From the way you talk it seems you've decided to stay on here and run the school.' Her eyes moved furtively over the instrument panel, the steering column, the wheel with long-fingered hands resting on its rim, moving on to his chest, his chin and settling at last on his face. 'Have you?' she whispered.

Against the background of their passengers' noise, Craig asked, with a hint of a smile, 'You'd like me to?'

'Yes.' The word was spoken on an expulsion of breath, full of hope and a betraying longing.

Now he stared through the windscreen, but it was plain he was seeing nothing beyond it. 'I haven't come to a decision one way or the other.'

'Oh.' Her voice was flat and she started to get out, but his hand reached for hers and covered it. It was a gesture of reassurance.

'I won't keep you—or Janine—long in suspense. I know how much you're involved with the place, how much you have at stake. As soon as I've made up my mind, I'll tell you.'

She slid her hand from under his. 'Thanks for your consideration.' The words were more edged than she had intended. It was obvious from his frown that they did not please him.

She asked dully, 'Can you manage the boys or do you want me to come with you to help sort them out?'

'No, thanks. Matron will take over.' His tone was as edged

173

as hers.

Had she really slept beside this man last night? Had his arms really held her, crushing her to him? Or had it all been a dream?

Janine welcomed Shelley as though she had been away for four months instead of four days. She commented with a laugh on Shelley's odd style of dress but did not wait for an explanation. She was too full of her own news.

'Shelley darling,' she said with an unaccustomed rush of sisterly feeling, 'he says he loves me. Marius wants me to marry him! I can't believe it. He says if I like he'll buy me out of Mrs. Caversham's and give Craig his money back. Then he'll give me the money to start a hairdressing business of my own in the town.' She frowned and pouted a little. 'Don't look at me as though you don't believe a word I'm saying. It's true, Shelley, all of it.'

Shelley felt for a chair and used it. 'I—don't really—doubt it for a moment, Jan,' she spoke slowly, 'but you must realise it's a bit of a shock. Jan, Marius's family—won't it go against the grain for them to have to welcome into it a comparatively penniless young woman—and someone as ordinary as a hairdresser?'

Janine dismissed her sister's anxieties at once. 'He's not *that* sort of a person, Shelley. He's not one of the old school aristocrats. He goes on demonstrations and marches and things. He's really terribly democratic.'

He must be, Shelley thought wryly, to get serious enough to want to marry a girl with such an unpretentious background as Jan's. 'He may be democratic, Jan, but his parents, what about them?'

'I've met them,' Janine said carelessly. 'They've got some sort of title. But it doesn't worry me.'

Shelley laughed. 'Maybe not, but do *you* worry *them*?'

Janine shrugged. 'All I can tell you is that they said to my face what a nice, level-headed sort of girl I seemed to be. And Marius told me afterwards that they were relieved to hear that their son had the sense to fall for a girl with her wits about her and who, they were sure, wasn't just after his money, like so many of his women acquaintances. What more can you want?'

Shelley felt reassured at last. It seemed that everything was falling into place for Janine, if not for herself. She told her sister that she was delighted to hear the news and asked how soon the engagement ring would be adorning her finger.

'In a few weeks. We're going to buy it together just before the announcement in the press.'

Announcement in the press? My word, Shelley thought, the younger Miss Jenner is certainly moving into exalted circles!

'They said,' Janine broke into her thoughts, 'they want to meet you. So does Marius.'

'I'm honoured,' said Shelley, with a touch of sarcasm.

'They're not like that at all,' Janine protested, and Shelley, sensing her sister was a little hurt, hugged her and said she was truly delighted to hear how well things were working out for her.

They talked then about other matters and Shelley asked about Emery. 'Gone home,' Janine told her. 'He went off in a huff because of the way Craig took his place on the camping expedition.' After that they discussed the storm and the havoc it had created over the countryside.

Then came the question Shelley had been dreading. 'When your tent collapsed, where did you spend the rest of the night?'

Shelley could not meet her sister's eyes. 'In Craig's tent.'

Janine's eyes rounded. 'So you slept together?'

'Don't be silly, Jan. You know I'd never——'

Janine laughed. 'No, I know you wouldn't. So does Craig. He once said that any man who wanted to get fresh with you would have to take a blowlamp and burn a path through the layers of ice that had formed around your primitive responses before he could even make first base!'

Shelley, sick at heart, went into the kitchen to get a meal. But why, she asked herself, get upset at hearing from Janine's lips what she already knew—that for Craig Allard she held no appeal, no attractions at all? Hadn't he told her so only that morning in a few blunt, well-chosen and contemptuous words?

175

Shelley went into work next day. She thought she would have the office to herself, and was intending to work her way through the piles of documents and letters that would be awaiting her.

But she was not alone for long. Craig came in. He was in a brisk, no-nonsense state of mind, and with a flick of the finger motioned her out of the 'hot seat', as he continued to call it, and took his place there instead.

Upset by the abrasiveness of his mood, she said, 'I was only trying to help. You might at least thank me——'

With a deep, mocking bow, he thanked her. 'Now let me have some peace and quiet so that I can study this—this——' He waved his hand over the piles of papers.

'Rubbish?' Shelley supplied sweetly.

'Rubbish,' Craig echoed, with a sarcastic smile. 'The word eluded me. Can you occupy yourself for the next half hour?'

'Easily.'

'Then get on with it.'

Shelley gave him an indignant look, but it made no impression.

Half an hour later he pushed the papers away with a movement of disgust, ran his hands through his hair, then supported his head on them. Had she, Shelley thought miserably, really been hoping Craig would somehow reconcile himself to becoming the head of Mapleleaf House School? To give up a good, intellectually challenging job at the university and taking on the running of a privileged school for equally privileged small boys?

For a long time, for as long as Craig sat with his head in his hands, Shelley kept her hands in her lap, clasping them and staying motionless. She knew Craig was thinking deeply. She believed he was engaged in a struggle—with his conscience, with the choice that lay before him, with the course of his whole future career.

She wished she could help him. She wished she could stand beside him, wind her arms round his neck, offer him comfort and loving advice.

'Craig?' she dared to whisper at last.

'Yes?' The reply was curt and he did not raise his head.

'What are you going to do?' Her voice sounded small and feeble.

'I don't know. If I did, I'd tell you.'

'I'm sorry.' But her apology went unheeded.

Tears started to her eyes, tears at his uncommunicativeness, at the formidable barriers dividing them, at the way he was shutting her out of his mind. Was she to have no say in the matter? And after all she had done for the school in his mother's frequent absences?

He got up and walked to the window, staring out at the trees and plants in full and fragrant bloom, at the gardeners at work on the flower beds, the handful of boys who, awaiting their parents' arrival, were playing on the large lawn.

'Craig?' Still he did not turn round. 'Do you know about Jan and Marius Halliday?'

'Yes. Janine phoned me. The receiver nearly bubbled in my ear with her enthusiasm for her new-found love.' He paused, then, 'When they marry, what will you do?'

Shelley answered carefully. 'That depends on you.'

He turned at last, slowly, suspiciously. 'What do you mean, "depends on me"?'

'If you give up the school, I'll have no job, no home.'

'I'm aware of that. Which makes it all the harder to come to a decision.' His expression grew sardonic. 'If I decided to opt out of the whole set-up, I'd have to throw out of her home a girl I've slept with.' His smile taunted. 'Since she gave me so much, the decision to deprive her of a roof over her head becomes very difficult to take.'

She coloured deeply. 'You know what you're saying is quite untrue.'

He strolled to her side. 'Is it?' He pulled her to her feet and kissed her lightly two or three times on the mouth. 'You gave me warmth and comfort when I needed it, you prevented me from suffering from exposure. Was that nothing?' She could not answer because his lips held hers again and this time his arms held her too, cradling her, tipping back her head.

He looked into her face. 'I owe you something for being caught up in the web of my mother's administrative incompetence.' He saw her frown and asked, 'You don't know what I mean? The old tent you had to sleep in, and its collapse.'

Shelley could not speak, she could only lie in his arms, animated, vibrant, waiting for his next kiss. She knew he was playing with her, that he did not—never would—take her seriously. But she also knew—deep in her heart she acknowledged the inevitable—that before many weeks had passed he would be gone, out of her life, as if he had never existed. If he was prepared to give her his kisses now, even though they were given carelessly, thoughtlessly, she would accept them with eagerness, and with thanks, as a starving man reaches out for a gourmand's left-overs.

But he did not kiss her again. Instead he put her away from him and asked, 'Will you dine with me tonight?'

'You mean—go out with you?'

'Why not? We could talk about the future.'

Her hopes, having risen to the heights, fell like a burnt out rocket. He did not seek her company, only her help in making up his mind.

'Thanks, Craig, I'd like to.' And if ever, she thought, there was an understatement, that was one.

'Good.' He returned to his desk. 'As I see it, I have a number of alternatives. Take on the job of running the place myself, or appoint a new head teacher and return to the university, letting him get on with it. I could put up the fees—an absolute "must" if the school is to continue to run effectively and competently. I could introduce modern thinking, modern techniques into the teaching of the children.' He drummed on the desk. 'It might—just—be a challenge. Anyway,' his face was illuminated with a smile which had Shelley's heart vibrating, 'this evening you can help me decide. You agree?'

'I agree,' she whispered.

He laughed. 'You said that as if you were taking the marriage vow. You came near to it once, didn't you?'

'Perilously near,' she answered, with a strained smile.

He looked at her curiously, but she did not answer the question in his eyes.

178

CHAPTER ELEVEN

SHELLEY borrowed a dress of Janine's to wear that evening. It was long and filmy and brilliantly patterned. She asked Janine to arrange her hair-style and when her sister had finished, Shelley thought that even Craig would not be able to overlook the fact that she was a woman—a warm, attractive woman—despite all his insulting remarks on the subject in the past.

He would probably never invite her to dine with him again. Why should he when, after this evening and he had come to his decision, they would not have to discuss the future any more? And that was the whole object of this outing with him, wasn't it?

She put on a necklace which Michael had given her. It was an amethyst and moonstone pendant on a gold chain. It had been lying in its box since the day Michael had gone out of her life.

The door knocker sounded and Shelley, panicking, called to Janine to answer it. 'Ask Craig in,' she called. 'Tell him I won't be long.'

There were voices in the entrance hall and Janine's was raised excitedly. Shelley thought, Jan must be telling Craig about Marius. A flick of the comb through her hair and Shelley was ready.

'Shelley! *Shelley!*' Janine's voice was urgent, compelling. 'Come on *down*, Shelley!'

Why, Shelley thought, is she getting so excited about Craig?

'You've got a visitor,' Janine was calling.

Shelley said from the landing, 'I know. I told you Craig was——'

'It's *not* Craig—it's—it's——'

A man appeared in the living-room doorway. His hair was brown and it trailed his collar. A moustache, a new addition to his long, angular face, decorated his upper lip.

179

Shelley, standing in the hall, held her breath. It could not be true! He had not come back. It was an illusion ... She whispered, unbelieving, '*Michael!*'

He went towards her, arms outstretched, and it was as if she were seeing a ghost from the dark corridors of her mind moving into the fierce light of day—a ghost that did not melt away but had solidity and substance. He was only a little taller than she was. In that he had not changed. But his manner, apologetic and uncertain, had altered beyond recognition. Where was the self-assurance, the too-confident smile, the near-salesman-like ability he possessed to sell himself to strangers?

'Shelley?' He took her hands. 'You look great, darling, just great. I've never seen you looking so beautiful.' His hands lifted and touched her throat. She might have been made of stone for all the effect his touch had on her. 'You're wearing my necklace! That's an encouragement in itself. It must prove I have a chance.' He kissed her cheek then, gently, asking, 'May I?' her lips. 'I've come to say I'm sorry and will you have me back?'

Shelley had no words with which to answer him.

'It was all a terrible mistake, Shelley, one I hope I'm still lucky enough to put right.' He put his arms about her and kissed her, experimentally the first time, then with greater assurance.

'Shelley,' Janine said, with uncharacteristic uncertainty in her voice, 'Craig's here.'

Shelley pulled herself from her ex-fiancé's embrace and swung round. How long had Craig been standing in the doorway? What had he seen? Everything, it appeared from the expression on his face. Shelley had been too shocked to hear his arrival. Every other thought had been wiped clean from her mind. For a few seconds an odd kind of amnesia had blotted out the present and only the past had remained.

Now she was back and the problems that confronted her had her reeling.

Michael was saying, 'Come out for a meal with me, darling.' What right had he, she thought angrily, to call her 'darling?' 'We've so much to talk about, so much catching up to do.'

180

'Michael, I can't.' The words came out hoarsely and she twisted round to face the man who stood watching the scene with sardonic eyes. 'Craig's taking me——'

'Forget it,' Craig said. 'Go out with your fiancé. I've plenty of work to keep me occupied.' He turned to go.

Shelley broke away and ran after him. 'Craig——' Anything to keep him there. 'Meet Michael Townley, my——'

'Her fiancé,' Michael put in, his self-confidence bounding back at Shelley's lack of repulse. 'You are——?' He was back on form, but the outstretched hand was ignored and the salesman's smile elicited a barely pleasant reply.

'The name is Allard, Craig Allard.'

'My employer's son,' Shelley explained, smiling so brightly it hurt her face. 'I'm dining——'

'Please forget it,' said Craig. Seconds later he had gone.

'Michael,' she said accusingly, 'it was wrong of you to assume we can turn back the clock and just go on from where we left off. I'm a different person——'

'You're so right, darling. I must have been crazy to walk out on you. I've hardly had a moment's peace——'

'How's Susanne?'

He looked a little shamefaced. 'Couldn't tell you. Haven't seen her for weeks. It's all finished.'

'So you've come back to me?'

Michael, failing to detect the sarcasm, plainly regarded the question as a form of encouragement. 'I've never really left you, darling. You stayed in my mind and I couldn't get you out.'

Smooth phrases, Shelley thought, looking into his face and wondering how she had ever thought she was in love with him. *Craig, she must put things right with Craig . . .*

'Jan,' Shelley called. Janine appeared from the kitchen. 'Talk to Mike for a few moments, will you? I—I want to make a phone call.'

Janine, puzzled, led Michael into the living-room and closed the door. Shelley dialled and drummed her fingers, waiting. At last the call was answered.

'Craig? Shelley here. Please, Craig, I don't want to dine with Michael. You asked me first——'

'Don't give it another thought. Regard the invitation as

cancelled. Better still, as though it had never been given.'

'But, Craig, please . . .'

'Don't you understand? I don't want your company.' He cut himself off.

Michael, over dinner in a local hotel, took a great deal of convincing that the girl he had been going to marry nearly a year before had had such a change of heart she was as good as telling him she didn't want to see him again.

Shelley tried to be polite, but if she was hurting him she did not care. He had hurt her immeasurably in the past. Could she be blamed if she indulged in just a little revenge? When Michael took her home, he was still unable to believe that her rejection was final.

'I understand,' he said. 'You're playing the game of having your own back. All right, salve your pride. But I'll be back, darling. Now I've found you again, now I've seen you as you really are, a beautiful, desirable woman, you think I'm going to let you go as easily as that?'

With a confident wave, he drove back to the hotel at which he was spending the night. As his car disappeared into the darkness, Shelley made for the phone. She dialled, hoping Craig had not gone out.

'Allard here,' the voice snapped.

'Craig, it's Shelley,' she said breathlessly. 'I'm home again. I phoned to say how sorry I am——'

'Spare me that,' came the clipped, cold reply. 'I don't want your apologies. I've been stood up before. I'm no stranger to the ways of women.'

'Craig, I didn't cancel the invitation. It was you——'

'Just why have you phoned? To let me know you're home before midnight? That you said, "No, Michael" like a good little girl and off he trotted, tail between his legs? So what does that prove? He'll be back tomorrow begging on the doorstep, and next time he may be more successful in his strategy and get what he wants without having to coax you into the mood by giving you a meal first.'

'Craig,' she cried, 'you're so wrong. I *wanted* to go out with you. We were going to discuss the future, remember——'

'As it happens, there's no need. I've come to a decision

without the expense of paying for a meal for two.'

Shelley sat on the stairs, her legs weak. 'You've decided? What—what have you decided, Craig?'

There was a long silence.

'Please tell me, Craig.' More silence. 'Please, Craig,' in a whisper, 'so much depends on your decision.'

'I'll see you in the morning.' There was a gloating note in his voice, as if he knew how much he was tantalising her.

'But, Craig, I won't sleep. I know I won't, if you don't tell me now.'

'Too bad. Think about your loved one. Maybe you'll dream you're in his arms, with or without that ring on your finger. What does it matter these days?'

With which cynical comment he ended the conversation.

Craig was at his desk next morning. When Shelley arrived he was reading the mail which he had opened himself, instead of waiting for her to do it.

When she said 'good morning' to his bent head, he did not raise it but nodded indifferently. She had intended asking him immediately what his decision had been about the future of the school, but his unapproachable mood intimidated her. And he did not voluntarily enlighten her.

Half the morning went by and the agony of having to stay silent was becoming unbearable. It was lunchtime before Shelley had gathered sufficient courage to confront him at his desk and ask, with a waver in her voice,

'What have you decided, Craig?'

He looked at her for the first time that day and she winced at the coldness in his eyes. 'I can't see that it's any concern of yours now what decision I've come to.' As if he hadn't humiliated her enough, he added, 'In any case, you're just the secretary around here, nothing more. Remember that.'

Just the secretary, she thought achingly, when I've spent a night in your arms?

He looked at his watch. 'It's lunchtime. You can go.'

'I don't want to go. I'm not hungry,' she cried, forced into losing her self-restraint by his callous indifference to her fate. 'How could I be when I don't know where I'll be living in a few weeks' time?'

He glanced up at her with surprise, and there was a question in his raised eyebrows.

'You must know what I mean,' she pressed on. 'If you sell the school, you'll be selling my home with it, and depriving me of my livelihood. I don't know how you can sit there so calmly, so—so *unfeelingly*, knowing that if you give up the school, you'll be making me homeless.'

'I know now, don't I? You've just told me.'

She could not stand his sarcasm at such a time. 'What are you going to do?' she repeated. But he was silent. Maddened, she pounded the desk with the palm of her hand. 'If you don't tell me,' she cried, 'I'll—I'll——'

'Resign?' Now the eyebrows were high and indifferent. 'Go ahead. It will save me the trouble of giving you notice.'

Shelley paled and put a shaking hand to her throat. 'You're—you're closing the school?'

He answered flatly, 'I'm closing the school. Not selling it, closing it.'

'And,' she whispered, 'the house?'

He lifted his shoulders. 'My mother told me she has no intention of living here with my new stepfather, in which case I'll probably sell the house, too.' He rose. 'So now you know.' He glanced at his watch. 'If you're not hungry, I am. If you'll excuse me ...'

She raced to the door and reached it before him, standing with her back to it. 'Why not sell the school?' she pleaded. 'There must be someone wanting to buy an establishment like this with a good reputation.'

'Thus keeping a roof over your head?' She nodded eagerly. 'Why should you worry now?'

'Why should I worry?' she responded, bewildered. 'When my home and future are threatened?'

'Like Janine's, your future's been taken care of. Jan's getting married. Your much-loved ex-fiancé has come back into your life and from the way he was kissing you and petting you yesterday, intends to stay there. Now will you let me pass?'

So he thought she had taken Michael back! Understanding how his mind was working at last, she shook her head.

184

He took the movement as a refusal to obey his request. His lips thinned, his hands gripped her shoulders and he swung her round, putting her behind him, but before he could reach the door Shelley grasped his arm and clung to it.

'Craig, Craig, listen to me!'

He tried to shake her off, but she put herself in front of him and caught his other arm. He looked down into her up-turned, appealing face, but his glance did not soften. Instead he smiled sardonically.

'What are you after? You want two men in tow? Aren't you satisfied with the one you've got? You want a little supplementary lovemaking because your boy-friend can't deliver the goods? That's fine with me. I'll oblige. God knows, you're giving me enough encouragement.'

His arms went round her, rough and ungentle, his lips thirsting and harsh, drawing the life from her. His hands tugged her blouse free of her skirt and his palms slipped, feather-light, over the bareness of her skin, fondling, stroking, exploring . . .

She clung with all her strength, giving as he gave, re-acting instinctively to his demands, his kisses on her body, her throat, her mouth. When his head lifted at last, his anger had not diminished. 'By the way you've been re-sponding, it seems I was right. Your boy-friend must be a weakling, a complete ignoramus on the subject of making love. I'll have to give him some lessons some time.' He must have seen the colour drain from her face, but his man-ner did not soften. 'Now you've got what you've been ask-ing for, perhaps you'll let me go.'

'Craig,' she whispered, her body throbbing, her limbs shaking, 'Craig——'

But he removed her clinging hands and sprinted up the stairs, putting the maximum distance between them in the shortest possible time. She was after him at once, two flights, three flights, four, gasping when she reached the top and hammering on his door.

'Craig,' she shrieked, 'let me in! Please, *please* let me in!' The door remained as implacable and unyielding as the man inside the room.

She twisted and rattled the handle. 'Craig, listen to me.

I'm not marrying Michael. I don't love him, Craig. I sent him away, I sent him away . . .' There was no movement, no sound in response to her words. Her fists pounded the obdurate door. 'Let me in, Craig, I want you!'

Hopeless now, she turned away, hands covering her face. Before she could go down those four flights of stairs, her eyes must clear, her head must stop reeling.

The key grated, the door swung open. Shelley turned, without eagerness. In his present mood, he probably had every intention of throwing her down the stairs.

But his mood seemed, incredibly, to have altered. His hand came out, fastened on to her arm and pulled her into the room. He stood with his back to the closed door, as if to ward off any attempt on her part to escape.

'Say that again,' he said.

'Say what again, Craig?' she asked, puzzled by the curious smile on his face. 'That I'm not marrying Michael? That I've sent him away?'

'You said something else. Say it again,' he repeated.

'I said,' she ran her tongue over her lips, 'let me in, Craig. I—I want you.'

His smile held victory, achievement, delight. He reached out for her, pulling her hard against him. 'At last she's done it! She's broken through those barriers, all of them, every single one. She's put aside her pride and her dignity. She's run after a man—four flights, four breathless flights of stairs—and she's told him she wants him!'

Aghast, she said, straining away from him, 'I don't mean it that way, Craig——' But, she asked herself, didn't she? Of course she wanted him, more than she had ever wanted Michael, more than any man in the whole world!

His lips trailed her eyes, her cheeks, her ears, where he whispered, 'And you shall have me, my sweet one, you shall have me for the rest of your life.'

His kisses came again and again, and in between were endearments, murmured, repeated, stroking her ears and her mind into tranquillity, her limbs into an unresisting compliance. At last he stopped and Shelley gazed up at him a little reproachfully.

'You made me do it,' she protested, 'you made me run

186

after you.' But her eyes were shining.

'Yes, I made you do it—in the end. There were times when I almost gave up in despair. But I forced you out of the darkness of that damned impregnable castle you'd withdrawn yourself into. I made you come out into the sunlight again. Admit you love me,' he shook her a little, 'admit it. You love me.'

But she did not care how much she told him now. He had read her mind in her actions, there was no sense in holding back. This man, she knew, would never let her down as Michael had done. 'I love you,' she whispered, 'oh, Craig, I love you ...'

'You trust me implicitly? You put yourself and your future in my hands?' She nodded. 'I wondered how long,' he murmured, his eyes scanning every detail of her face, 'it would take me to get that out of you. Ever since the day I met the girl with another man in her mind, I've been trying to coax her into falling in love with me. Everything I've said and done in your presence has been calculated to that end. Do you know something? I fell in love with the girl with the faraway look in her eyes. From the moment I met you I became jealous of that man you were thinking about.'

'But, Craig,' her hands rested against his chest, 'how can you say that? You were friendly with Jan——'

'Friendly is the right word, sweet. It was nothing more. She often told me on our outings that I bored her with my wisdom and my "superior" knowledge, as she called it. If you'd had eyes in your head, eyes that looked outward instead of inward, you would have seen months ago which sister I really wanted. The older, not the younger; the beautiful, not the pretty one, the one with intelligence and wisdom and everything a man could ask for. Why do you think I gave Jan that money if not to take some of the weight off your shoulders? Why do you think it took me so long to make up my mind about the school? Because the thought of leaving you behind and never seeing you again was driving me slowly mad.'

'But, Craig, I stopped loving Michael months ago. Since I met you, I think——'

'Yet when I asked you that day if you'd take him back if

he ever returned to you, you said you didn't know.'

She put her cheek against his shoulder. 'Of course I knew, but I wasn't going to tell you!'

'You minx!' He kissed her again. Then she asked,

'If you felt like that about me, Craig, why did you hold back that night in the tent?'

He lifted her chin. 'What a question! What did you honestly expect me to do? Take you by force, make you mine brutally, without finesse, without tenderness? If I'd loved you less, maybe I would have done. But the depth of my feeling for you kept my desire under control—just.' He smiled. 'Although if you'd given me one sign, one single sign of your feelings for me, it would have opened the floodgates and I can assure your our relationship would have been very different after that!'

Shelley stroked his cheek and he groaned and crushed her to him. 'My love,' he whispered hoarsely, 'marry me quickly. Don't try me too far. My barriers are cracking under the strain. I can wait a few days, no more. Are you agreeable?'

'Why not?' she whispered back. 'I'm not a very patient person, either, especially where the man I love is concerned.'

He pulled her against him and for a long time there was no need for words.

Shelley asked at last, 'Where shall we live? Are you still returning to your job?'

He nodded. 'I have a flat near the university. We'll live there until we find ourselves a house.'

'So you really are closing the school?'

'Do you mind?'

'Not now.' Her hands smoothed the back of his head. 'It was the thought of being parted from you that terrified me. This house, Craig—will you give it up?'

He smiled. 'You want me to keep it?'

Shelley nodded. 'I've grown to love it. For some reason,' her eyes laughed up at him, 'it has such happy associations for me.'

'Then we'll keep it in the family. We'll spend our holidays here, bring our children——'

Her fingers rested on his mouth. 'You're going too fast!' He laughed and kissed the fingers. She smiled at him provocatively. 'Aren't you breaking your own rules? You told me so often you didn't believe in marriage.'

His fingers grasped her chin. 'Look at me like that much longer, my darling, and I'll break some other rules, too. I won't wait...'

The noise of the lunch bell, ringing in the distance, brought them down to earth.

As they strolled to the door, arms round each other, Craig said, 'Do you want to know when I started to believe in marriage? The day I met you. The moment I saw you, spectacles and all, and with man-hate in your eyes, I knew you were the one woman I wanted to have and to hold until death us did part. My love,' he drew her away from the door and back into his arms, 'it was you, and only you, who turned me into the marrying kind.'

Harlequin

the unique monthly magazine packed with good things for Harlequin readers!

A Complete Harlequin Novel

You'll get hours of reading enjoyment from Harlequin fiction. Along with a variety of specially selected short stories, every issue of the magazine contains a complete romantic novel.

Readers' Page

A lively forum for exchanging news and views from Harlequin readers. If you would like to share your thoughts, we'd love to hear from you.

Arts and Crafts

Unusual handicraft articles are a fascinating feature of Harlequi magazine. You'll enjoy making your own gifts an indulging your creativity when you use these alway clear and easy-to-follow instructions.

Author's Own Story . . .

Now, meet the very real people who create the romantic world of Harlequin! In these unusual author profiles a well-known author tells you her own personal story.

Harlequin Cookery

Temptingly delicious dishes, plain and fancy, from all over the world. Recreate these dishes from tested, detailed recipes, for your family and friends.

Faraway Places . . .

Whether it's to remind you of places you've enjoyed visiting, or to learn about places you're still hoping to see, you'll find the travel articles informative and interesting — and just perfect for armchair travelling.

Harlequin